Gooney Bird

By

Rick Byam

To: Clathy   August 2003

Thanks for supporting this venture.

Enjoy the ride!

Rick

ISBN: 1-4107-3871-X (E-book)
ISBN: 1-4107-3870-1 (Paperback)

Library of Congress Control Number: 2003092267

This book is printed on acid free paper.

Printed in the United States of America
Bloomington, IN

1st Books - rev. 4/12/03

Appreciation

Many thanks to Kevin Uppstrom for giving me the opportunity to fly the DC-3 and for his technical assistance on this project. Thanks to Steve Cook for teaching me how to fly the "Gooney." Special thanks to Maggie Ward, Lorna Beyer, Nancy Russell, Carol Byam, Marge Cooley, and Sue and Bob Donoghue for taking the time to read the manuscript and offer their comments and opinions. A gracious and heartfelt thanks to my editor, Peg Hagar, for her support and editing skills throughout the final stages of preparing the manuscript.

Dedication

This book is dedicated to everyone who looks to the skies for adventure.

Part I

Rick Byam

ONE

MJ was running back toward the cockpit when the plane suddenly shuddered and there was a loud noise from underneath her feet. Through the side windows she saw an F-16 fly from underneath the plane, round out, and begin another pass at her big, beautiful Gooney Bird. She strapped herself in, flipped the transponder to 7500, indicating a hijacking was taking place, and dialed the emergency frequency, 121.5, into the #1 radio.

"DON'T SHOOT! JESUS CHRIST, DO NOT SHOOT! THIS PLANE IS FULL OF CHEMICALS! DON'T SHOOT!" she screamed into her microphone.

She watched as the F-16 completed its course reversal and leveled itself at the DC-3.

"DO YOU HEAR ME? DON'T SHOOT, GODDAMMIT! THE PLANE'S FULL HAZARDOUS MATERIALS!"

The F-16 headed directly at her, but she didn't dare take any evasive action for fear they would construe it to be an aggressive or non-compliant maneuver. The Falcon screamed over the top of the Gooney bird so close that MJ thought it was going to hit her. The vortices from the speeding jet rocked the DC-3, and MJ had to fight for control.

"November one eight Mike Juliet, the DC-3 just south of Midway Field. This is Lightning Strike Leader at your six-o'clock. Do you copy?" the voice on the radio said.

"I HEAR YOU! I HEAR YOU! DO NOT SHOOT! THIS PLANE IS FULL OF HAZMAT! IF WE GO DOWN, A LOT OF PEOPLE ARE

4

GOING TO DIE! DO YOU HEAR *ME*?" she
yelled into the microphone.

"This was NOT part of my business
plan," she thought, as she fought to
keep the Gooney Bird under control.

TWO

Although MJ had just celebrated her thirty-sixth birthday, most people thought she was still a teenager and were surprised when they saw her emerge from the freight doors of the vintage DC-3. They were downright flabbergasted when they found out she was the captain.

She was tall and slender, and the cold climate of her Montana home kept her skin healthy and smooth. Her blue eyes and blonde hair hinted at her Scandinavian ancestry, but the stubborn and fearless nature of her being was the result of the

6

Native American Blackfoot blood that coursed through her veins. Being the youngest in the family with three older brothers to contend with didn't do her any harm, either. She had learned to hold her own and was known to have gotten a brother or two out of a scrape with her feminine ferocity. It was this unique recipe that got MJ into aviation. She feared nothing and wanted the freedom and independence that flying had to offer.

As soon as she turned sixteen, MJ started working the line for Jacob's Mountain Flying Service at Big Timber Field. The airport was about sixty miles west of Billings, Montana and had a single, 5300' runway. She saved enough money in six months to begin taking flying lessons and spent every spare moment studying the texts and manuals for the private pilot certificate. She soloed after eight flights and completed the rest of the requirements in less than thirty-seven hours of flight time, well below the norm. She scheduled her check ride for the morning of her seventeenth birthday and was giving rides to her brothers, mother, and father that afternoon.

Big Timber didn't have a published instrument approach procedure, so MJ drove the twenty miles west to Mission Field for her instrument training. Since it was summer and the days were longer, she worked for Jacob from 6 a.m. until 3 p.m., then drove to Mission Field and put in a couple of hours of training. Once she had the basic dual instruction out of the way, she teamed with another instrument pilot trainee who had his own plane and kept it at Big Timber. This saved her the forty-mile drive to and from Mission and some hard-earned cash, as she only had to pay for the fuel for her leg of the practice sessions. MJ had her instrument ticket in six weeks and began her commercial training immediately.

After graduating from high school, Mary Jane took a job working the line for a company at Billings' Logan International Airport. They also had her flying bank checks and receipts at night, helping her build time as a commercial pilot and earn the money she would need to pay for her multiengine rating. She usually finished her route and was back on the field by 1 a.m., and her apartment was a convenient ten minutes away, making it easy to get home and get some sleep before starting it all over again. Because she was doing both jobs, the owners had her start her day at 10 a.m., giving her a little more time to rest before the next grueling ordeal began. She had no social life and paid that no mind; flying was her passion. That's all she needed. That's all she wanted.

In just over a year, MJ earned her multiengine ticket and accumulated a significant number of hours flying skydivers and bank statements. She was constantly searching the trades for a job that would move her career forward and applied for all the jobs that even came close to her qualifications. She sent the appropriate paperwork, had an occasional interview, and made the follow-up call, only to hear a bored voice tell her that they weren't interested. There was always a lack of something: not enough total time, not enough multiengine time, not enough instrument time, not enough lunar landings. Whatever! The final blow came when she was turned down by a company in Detroit and then found out, through a pilot friend, that they hired a male with much less experience for the same job. The one thing that she didn't plan on was rearing its ugly head; she was a woman! When it came time to move into the better and higher paying jobs, she hit the glass ceiling. Until that moment, it didn't even cross her mind. Now she saw it everywhere she looked. "There is a reason it's called the cockpit," she complained.

THREE

Mary Jane didn't consider herself particularly religious, but she liked to go to church functions to stay in touch with the folks she grew up with in McLeod, Montana, a small town on the Boulder River. It was during one of these events that she finally got a break. While lamenting the obstacles facing women pilots in a conversation with a former classmate, the local pastor, Nelson Herring, interrupted her. He smiled when she looked at him.

"Hi, Mary Jane. I don't mean to be rude or intrusive," he said, "but I

11

heard from your folks that you're having a bit of trouble finding the kind of job you'd like, and you're running into a 'good old boy' network. Maybe I can help. I've got a friend who is looking for a copilot to help with his missionary work, south of the border. It seems they use this big, old, ugly C-47, bought from the Salvadorian government, to ferry them around and help the people in remote areas. Because there's no money it, he has a hard time finding someone to fill the slot. Is this something that might interest you?"

"Are you kidding?" she shot back. "I would *love* to drive one of those Gooney Birds. Sign me up!"

"I think he's looking for a one year commitment. That might be another reason why he can't find anyone to go. Like I said, there's no money in it, but he will feed and house you. How's your Spanish?"

"I had two years in high school. I bet I can remember enough to keep myself out of trouble. How do I get in touch with this person?"

Nelson thought for a moment and then looked back at her.

"Give me a day or two. I think I might be able to get in touch with him without too much trouble. Here. Write down something about your flying experience that I can pass on to him; I'll see what I can do."

"Thanks, Nelson," she said, grinning from ear to ear. "You hook me up with this mission, and I'll never stiff the offering plate again."

"Really?" Nelson mused. "I'm not sure who's getting the better deal here, Mary Jane. Call me in a couple of days."

"You betcha!" she replied. "Count on it!"

FOUR

Nelson Herring kept his word. MJ hooked up with his missionary friend, Ned Greenlawn, over the telephone and made the deal that would put her behind the wheel of a DC-3. She tied up loose ends with her job, packed what she thought she would need into an old, army-surplus duffel bag, said goodbye to her family and friends, and began what she considered to be the adventure of a lifetime.

MJ took a flight from Billings to Dallas-Fort Worth and then switched to a direct flight to Mexico City.

For once, everything was on time.
The weather was clear, the flights
were smooth, and MJ Carlson was in
her element.

As the 727 began its descent into
Mexico City, MJ stared out the
window and marveled at the
landscape: tall mountains, plateaus,
and sparsely populated deserts
drifted past her window. It went by
so fast, however, that she had no
time to appreciate all it had to
offer. "That will change soon
enough," she said, under her breath.
"Once we start flying low and slow,
I'll see every nook and cranny in
this place."

As the large jet passed over the
rim of the extinct volcano that
houses Mexico City, the view took on
a different hue: the haze became
thicker and the visibility dropped
dramatically. MJ wondered if the
pilots were going to have to shoot
an instrument approach on this
otherwise bright and sunny day. She
watched the buildings of the city
come into view as the plane banked
and turned to various headings. She
envisioned the aircraft sequencing

with other traffic and aligning with the appropriate runway.

She thought back to her research on this large and diverse country and what she had read about Mexico City. The literature explained how the old walls of the volcano trap the air and prevent the prevailing winds from removing it from the sprawling city. And, with the increasing number of immigrants coming to the city looking for a better opportunity, the pollution was getting worse. As the plane passed over the outskirts of the city, MJ caught a glimpse of the shantytowns that seemed to extend to the horizon. She remembered reading about the wind and dust that blew through the city on a regular basis, carrying dried human excrement from the shantytowns that lacked running water and sewer systems. The people just used the open spaces. She wondered how people could live like that and maintain any kind of healthy existence, both in and out of the city. She also wondered just how much of the poverty and unhealthy living she was going to encounter as a missionary pilot.

"Ladies and gentlemen," the flight attendant said over the intercom. "The captain has turned on the seatbelt sign, indicating that we have begun our final approach into Mexico City. Please make sure that your seatbelts are securely fastened and that your tray tables and seat backs are in their upright and locked position. We will be coming through the aisles once more to collect any remaining items you wish to throw away. Thank you."

MJ checked her seatbelt, raised her seat, and went back to observing the foreign scene scrolling past her window. She heard the sound of electric motors and looked back over the wing to catch a glimpse of the initial deployment of the wing flaps. She went through her own mental checklist of things to be accomplished before an airplane could be safely planted back on the earth. She anticipated the next item on the pilots' checklist as they configured the aircraft for the final segment of the approach. The plane banked twice more and deployed flaps each time. MJ felt the floor shake as the gear doors opened into the slipstream and knew this would

Rick Byam

increase drag enough to require more
power to remain airborne. She felt
the "clump" of the gear in her feet
and legs as it locked into place,
and the seatbelt tugged at her as
the slowing jet forced her forward
in her seat. The final extension of
flaps and the spooling up of the
engines announced the imminent
reunion with terra firma. MJ rested
her head on the back of her seat and
watched the rest of the landing
through her window. The black
asphalt of the runway rushed past
the window; the airplane seemed to
float for some distance before the
wheels made contact with the
surface. The plane began to shake
and groan with the unhappy marriage
of rubber and asphalt. These
vehicles were made to fly, not to be
driven over bumps and dips of man-
made objects. MJ always thought the
planes were voicing complaints about
being on the ground when they
touched down and began the rollout.
The roar outside of the window
increased steadily as the pilot
applied the thrust reversers to the
large, silver jet. The extended use
of the TRs and heavy braking,
pushing MJ and her fellow passengers
harder against their seatbelts,

convinced her that they had, in fact, drifted a good distance down the runway before contacting the ground. The engine noise died as quickly as it had erupted and the brakes released, freeing the passengers from their strained condition. The aircraft exited the runway and began its migration to the terminal, where MJ was supposed to meet Ned in person for the first time.

Ned Greenlawn had already lived a lifetime as far as MJ was concerned. He had been a corpsman in the army during the Vietnam era, serving in the early seventies and receiving many purple hearts. He received the Congressional Medal of Honor for bravery under fire and helping hundreds of soldiers on the battlefield. As if that weren't enough, after returning to the US, he signed on with a company that was providing free medical care to the people living in remote areas of Central and South America. It was during this time that he had learned to fly the DC-3. One of the pilots in the organization took him under his wing, so to speak, and taught him how to handle the big Gooney

Bird. After a couple of years of driving the thing, they paid off a Colombian official to issue him a pilot's license, and no one had ever questioned him about it. Of course, like a driver's license, you never really need the thing until something goes wrong; then everybody wants to see every scrap of paperwork you own. The advantage to working in this part of the world is that the local currency, or US dollars, is really the only paperwork you'll ever need when you find yourself in a jam.

The aircraft came to its final resting-place at the gate; MJ unbuckled her seatbelt. She pulled her backpack from under the seat in front of her and waited for some of the passengers to clear the aisle before attempting to get her other carry-on from the overhead compartment. She took her place in the aisle and shuffled sideways along the skinny passageway behind the others. By the time she reached the front of the plane and the exit, she could feel the heat of the Mexican noonday sun. It overpowered the air-conditioning system of the plane and clawed its way past crew and passengers, attempting to engulf the entire cabin as quickly as possible. It was succeeding. MJ was sweating profusely by the time she stepped out of the door.

Although she didn't have a clear picture of what Ned looked like, she had formulated an image in her mind from the information gleaned from Herring and Ned's voice over the phone. She figured he was about fifty, a little heavy, and probably tan and wrinkled from all the time he'd spent in the jungles and hot sun. He had been very easy to talk to and laugh with, putting her immediately at ease. He told her to travel lightly and not to bring any electronic devices. (There were few places to plug them in, and the current was 220 volts rather than the usual 115 volts commonly used in the US.) She was to bring a Spanish dictionary, leave her prejudices—if she had any—in the US, and be prepared for the hardest thing she would probably ever do.

That statement almost changed her mind. She wanted to fly; that's all she cared about. If he was going to teach her how to fly the DC-3, and she was going to be able to fill her logbook, so be it. She was in. A year was just that: one year. She had already spent many difficult years getting to where she was, so one more wasn't going to stand in her way.

MJ and her fellow passengers flowed up the ramp and into the lounge, like so many cattle going to slaughter. She welcomed the cool breeze of the air-conditioned environment. Evidently, the sheer size of the building's cooling system was sufficient to ward off the oppressive heat that just about melted her in the companionway. She looked around for signs leading to the baggage claim, found one, and marched off to collect the duffel bag that contained all her possessions for the coming year.

Clearing customs was easier than she expected; no one inspected any of her bags. They asked for her passport, stamped it, asked the purpose of her visit—not even waiting for an answer—and waved her through. She guessed that either she didn't fit any of the profiles that would have required more scrutiny, or that the Mexican government wasn't all that concerned about who entered their country. Maybe it was just that she was clearly an American . . . and a woman. Welcome to Mexico!

MJ stepped into the main terminal and mayhem. There must have been a thousand people standing around waiting for friends and relatives to clear customs and join them. Many held up signs with names; they were hoping they could be quickly united with the arriving passenger and go on their way from this madhouse. MJ looked around for a face that might match the image of Ned she had formulated in her brain. About three rows back from the edge of the throng in front of her, she caught a glimpse of a sign that said "Carlson." She pushed her way through the crowd and stood in front of a small, dark, mustached man, grinning from ear to ear. He had a gold tooth, that seemed to be reflecting all the available light in the terminal, set squarely in the middle of his upper plate, and was trying desperately to look over the crowd in front of him, all of whom towered above him.

23

"I'm Mary Jane Carlson," she said, looking down at this, obviously, happy man. "You're not Ned, are you?"

"Señorita Carlson, la pilota?" he asked, looking up with an ever-widening grin.

"La pilota?" she thought and then remembered. "Pilot! Yes! I'm Señorita Carlson—the pilot. Did Mr. Greenlawn send you?" she asked.

"Señor Ned asked me to take you to the hotel," he answered. "My automobile is across the street, over by the park. Here, let me take something for you," choosing MJ's backpack over the bulky duffel bag.

"A wise choice," she thought, doubting he would be able to do anymore than drag the duffel along the floor, due to his proximity to the ground. She resigned herself to the task of lugging it herself and accepted his offer to help as he saw fit.

"My name is Rodrigo," he said, jabbing his index finger into his chest and grinning proudly at MJ. "I am Señor Ned's helper when he is in Mexico City. He had to pick up a lot of supplies for his next trip to the jungles, so he asked me to meet you."

"It's nice to meet you, Rodrigo," she said, matching her smile to his. "Most people call me MJ," as she pointed to herself and said the words slowly. "Did Señor Ned say when I would see him?" she inquired.

"Sí, Señorita. He say he will meet you for dinner at the hotel," Rodrigo answered. He pushed the revolving door of the airport terminal and led the way out and onto the sunny streets. "The car is about two blocks from here, over by the park."

They emerged from the terminal and were immediately greeted by the stifling heat of the day. MJ felt as though she was going to evaporate, as they walked the four blocks to the car.

Rodrigo was soon depositing her things next to an old Nissan Sentra that was parked next to a small botanical park. He gave the man leaning on the car some pesos, shook his hand, opened the door, and proceeded to load her things into the back seat. MJ followed suit and opened the back door on her side, stuffed her duffel bag into the back, pulled her wet blouse away from her clammy skin, and got into the passenger side of the Nissan. There wasn't a molecule of air to breathe.

The ride through the city was maddening. Rodrigo talked constantly as he weaved through traffic, dodged pedestrians, and zigzagged through neighborhoods and narrow streets. MJ understood less than half of what he was saying to her, as he mixed Spanish and English together. It was hard enough determining when he was talking to her and not to some driver or pedestrian who was running for his life and shaking a fist in Rodrigo's direction. MJ hung onto the door handle to maintain her balance and keep the door from swinging open. Rodrigo's car was meant for city driving: it was full of dents, the windshield wipers were non-existent, the windshield was cracked, and the only things that seemed to work were the engine and the radio . . . both quite loudly! MJ tried to take in some of the sights of the city but found that she couldn't really tell one part from the next; it appeared that Rodrigo was taking back streets to avoid the congestion on the main thoroughfares. She could see the main avenues in quick glimpses through the side streets and alleys, but decided that he definitely wasn't taking her on the standard tourist routes.

"Just a couple of more streets, Señorita MJ, and we'll be at the hotel! OK?" he yelled over his shoulder to her. He leaned on the horn and swerved to miss a car that was using the same side of the street as they were.

"Chingada Pendejo!" Rodrigo screamed at the offending driver, as their windows passed each other. He looked at MJ with his big grin and gold tooth and shrugged his shoulders. "Some people don't know how to drive in Mexico City," he explained.

"Obviously not," MJ agreed.

27

The car pulled up to the curb in front of a narrow, dirty, marble building. Rodrigo jumped from the car, grabbed the item he had put into the back seat, and headed for the front door.

"This is the hotel?" MJ asked, as she opened the backdoor of the car and dragged her duffel bag onto the pavement.

"Sí, Señorita. Don't worry; it's very nice. Cheap, too!"

"I'll bet," MJ offered, under her breath.

Once past the doors and through the narrow hallway, MJ could see that it was, in fact, nice. The polished, cherry reception desk was clean and orderly, as was everything else in sight. An archway framed an enclosed patio with tile floors and walls, a water fountain, plants, and flowers were everywhere. Someone was cooking, and she could smell the rich aroma of garlic, onions, and something else she didn't recognize.

"Buenas tardes, Señorita Carlson," the tall dark man behind the desk said, handing her a room key. "We have been expecting you. I hope that your journey was a pleasant one. Your room is on the second floor, down the hall to the right. Señor Greenlawn will be meeting you for dinner this evening. He said he will call you when he is finished with his business."

The man appeared formal in his presentation, but his dress was plain and simple. MJ thanked him and turned to Rodrigo.

"Do I owe you anything for the ride, Rodrigo?" she asked.

"Oh, no Señorita. Señor Ned has taken care of everything," extending his hand to her. "It's always my pleasure to help him, in any way I can, when he's in Mexico City. I hope you enjoy your stay; I will see you tomorrow."

MJ shook his hand and returned the smile.

"Gracias, Rodrigo," she said, using her limited Spanish for the first time.

"De nada, Señorita MJ. Hasta luego, Muchacha," he said, as he turned on his heel and walked down the narrow hallway toward the bustling streets that now seemed so far away from MJ.

FIVE

MJ descended the staircase slowly, holding on to the polished oak railing and looking at the Mexican landscape in the paintings that filled the wall on her left. Occasionally, she would stop and gaze at one in particular, tracing the form of the mountains with her fingertips and feeling the texture of the abundant paint on the canvas. Her long, slender legs slid smoothly beneath the flowered summer dress, as she daintily reached for the next step with her sandaled foot. As she made the turn to the final set of steps, she took in an elevated view

31

of the lobby with its crystal chandelier, tiled floor, and blue mosaic walls. Everything was spotless, and it was as quiet as a tomb. There was nothing like the chaos that reigned just outside the front door of the hotel. A different desk clerk was now sitting on a stool behind the white marble top of the reception desk, reading a paperback novel and sipping coffee from a china cup. The neat rows of pigeonholes behind him were more than half-filled with unclaimed room keys; a few of them had letters protruding, awaiting the expected return of a current resident or guest. The phone on the counter looked like something out of an Ozzie and Harriet episode from the 50s. The cash register was an antique, something you would see in a general store when you visited a heritage village with its relevant period pieces. Only here it wasn't on display as an antique; it was an integral part of the hotel.

Ned Greenlawn left a message that he would meet MJ at eight o'clock for dinner. She wanted to make sure he would be there when she came down, so she purposely arrived ten minutes late. It wasn't her custom to be late for meetings, but this was foreign to her, and she wasn't quite ready to go it alone. The desk clerk looked up from the book he was reading and gaped at the voluptuous figure standing before him. His jaw slackened as he filled his eyes with the fountain of beauty that bubbled before him. MJ had her hair back with a single hair-band, letting the long blonde strands fall onto her shoulders slightly forward of her collarbone. She didn't believe in makeup, so she wore none. Perfume made her gag, so she didn't have any on. The perfumed soap from her shower would have to do. The lack of these feminine amenities, however, didn't deter the clerk from his long gaze, so MJ decided to try her luck with some more ancient high school Spanish.

"Buenas noches, Señor."

The desk clerk snapped out of his hypnotic trance, put the book underneath the counter, stood up, and placed both hands on the marble top.

"Buenas noches, Señorita. You are looking very beautiful this evening."

"Gracias," she responded, blushing just a little as she arrived at the front desk.

"Señor Ned arrived a short while ago. He's waiting for you in the restaurant. Please, go right in. It's just through that doorway to your right," he said, as he leaned over the counter and pointed around the corner.

"Gracias," she acknowledged. It occurred to her that it wouldn't matter what language she used to speak to the man. He looked as if he were about to leap over the counter and do her bidding for the rest of his natural life . . . maybe longer.

"De nada, Señorita," he said. "If there is *anything* I can do for you, please don't hesitate to ask. I am Ramón. Ramón José Gutierrez Sanchez, a su servicio—at your service," he clarified in English.

"Gracias," she said, once more. "I appreciate that."

MJ turned the corner and passed through a dark wood archway that led her to the most beautiful courtyard she had ever seen. The floor was a maze of cobblestones with a myriad of what appeared to be ancient Aztec figures and designs. In the center of the courtyard stood a tall fountain with the figure of an Indian perched on the uppermost part. The Indian was holding something in each hand, and from these objects water flowed freely, filling the bowl that surrounded him. From there it flowed through four conch shells that were spaced evenly around the bowl and down into the next level. The process repeated itself four times, until the water reached the lowest level and emptied into a small pond with water lilies and goldfish that glided smoothly below the surface. Occasionally their dorsal fins interrupted the glassine sheen of the surface and created small ripples that gently rocked the lily pads. It was very serene.

The courtyard was open to the evening sky, and MJ could see that twilight had reached the city. There were wrought-iron supports on the walls, each holding a flaming torch. Flaming pots illuminated the walkways when the sun was no longer available. Each of the dozen or so tables held a candle in its center, adding to the ambiance. Ferns in hanging baskets suspended from the balcony above and exotic plants growing around the perimeter complimented the tranquil scene. MJ felt as though she had just stepped into the courtyard of some eighteenth century hacienda. She probably had, for all intents and purposes.

"You must be Mary Jane," said a voice from the edge of the courtyard.

MJ stepped back a pace and looked in the direction of the voice. She was so taken with the beauty of the courtyard she had forgotten why she came.

"Mr. Greenlawn?" she asked, as she tried to focus on the man in the torchlight walking toward her.

"Call me Ned, please. How are you? Did you have a good trip? Is everything satisfactory here at the hotel?"

"Uh, yes, yes. Everything's just fine," she stammered. "Um, the trip was fine, too. So am I," she tossed out as an afterthought. She reached out to take the hand that was offered.

Although not knowing what to expect, never having seen a picture, she was surprised to see that she was just about as tall as he was, and that he was so very thin. It looked as though he had his belt on the last loophole and could've used another one . . . or two. His salt-and-pepper hair was a bit mussed, but his beard was closely cropped, although not trimmed in any fashion. His warm brown eyes were smiling at her, along with a wide grin that flashed nearly perfect white teeth. MJ had expected a more tanned and muscled individual with a strong square chin. Other than the tan, she felt that he couldn't have been further from the mental image she held than if she had not formed an image at all. He looked healthy, but his skinny appearance made him look

frail. "Life is full of surprises,"
she thought.

"It's so nice to finally meet you,
Mary Jane. Nelson speaks very highly
of you," he said. He shook her hand
with both of his.

"Call me MJ. Everybody does," she
said in response. She noticed his
hands were callused and somewhat
thin; however, there was no
mistaking their strength.

"OK, MJ. Care for some dinner? I
took the liberty of ordering for
both of us. As you can see, there
aren't many people here, so we have
the kitchen and wait-staff to
ourselves. These folks know me from
the hundreds of times I've stayed
here, and some of them are here
because I brought them here. We
should be treated like royalty."

"That's fine with me," she said.
"I wouldn't know what to order
anyway. I mean, I've had Tex-Mex
before, but I've never had what I'd
call real Mexican food."

"You're in for a real treat. Most
people think Mexican food is all

spiced up and a real tongue burner. It just isn't so. Of course, you *can* get real spicy food if you want it; however, most of that is in the Yucatan or close to the US border. Here in the city, the food is just great: tasty, flavorful, sumptuous, yummy, and outrageous. It's the best."

MJ laughed at Ned's obvious love of the native cuisine and moved around the table to take her place in the seat he pulled out for her. He helped her move her chair closer to the table and went around to the other side to take his place. A woman dressed in native Mayan clothing came to the table with a bottle of wine. In her wake, she brought the strong smell of garlic, olive oil, and spices from the kitchen. She held the bottle for Ned's inspection. He nodded at the woman, and she opened the bottle and poured some into his glass. While she was waiting for his response, she turned MJ's wineglass over and then looked back at Ned.

"Muy bien," he assured the server.

She poured some wine into MJ's glass and then added more to his. She placed the bottle on the table to one side and returned to the kitchen to get warm tortillas and guacamole dip for their table. She was back in an instant and placed them between the two diners before retiring to the kitchen area, once again.

Ned lifted his glass toward MJ and said, "Salud!"

MJ lifted her glass and touched it to his. "Salud!"

They both took a sip from their glasses. MJ placed hers back onto the table; Ned rested his just below his lips with both hands.

"So, MJ. Are you ready for some serious flying?"

"I was watching the terrain as we flew toward the city," she said. "It looks quite diverse: deserts, mountains, plateaus, coastal flying down and dirty."

"Yes, Mexico has just about every type of terrain you could expect.

Where we're going, we'll be dealing with a lot of jungle, too."

"When we will get started?" she asked.

"Got to get right to it, eh?" he responded. "Well, you won't be disappointed, MJ. We leave Mexico City tomorrow morning, bright and early. Rodrigo will be by to pick you up at 5 a.m."

MJ picked up her glass of wine and took another sip.

"Five a.m.? Tomorrow?" she said, quite surprised.

"I said you wouldn't be disappointed. We have a lot to do, and hanging around the city won't get it done. Rodrigo will drop you off at a warehouse just southwest of the city. If everything goes as planned, I'll have our truck loaded by then, and we can scoot out of town as soon as you arrive. If not, you can help me finish loading the supplies. It'll be good practice for you. It seems I've been spending most of my life lately loading and unloading that big ugly bird. You

41

probably should wear a pair of long pants that you don't mind getting dirty, work boots if you have them, and some kind of hat. The sun gets pretty intense down here, even in the early morning hours. I keep plenty of work gloves on hand—I suspect you didn't bring your own—so that should work out. I guess that's enough of your initial briefing, for now. Any questions?"

MJ studied his face while he told her all this. She noticed numerous small scars among the tanned wrinkles. There was a large one that started near the corner of his left eye, went down over his left cheek, and disappeared behind his beard. She also noticed a slight trembling of his hands when he held his glass.

MJ had a million questions about everything, but figured she'd have a chance to ask them and have them answered over the next twelve months. She kept it simple.

"Where do we go tomorrow?"

"We'll take the highway toward Cuernavaca," he answered. "That's southwest of here. The plane is at a small dirt strip just south of Tepotzlan, about halfway between here and Cuernavaca. I prefer to use out-of-the-way airstrips when I can. It saves on the hassles with airport security, paying off the line guys to keep them from stealing our stuff, and paying the local authorities to keep them from hassling us about paperwork. Don't get me wrong. Everything's in order and on the up-and-up. Nevertheless, here in Mexico, everyone's looking for 'la mordida,' the bite. It's a way of life down here; you pay to get anything done. I pay just one guy to keep an eye on the plane and keep people away. Like all the private security people you see everywhere, he carries a shotgun and wears a semi-uniform: brown pants with a blue stripe down the side and a tan shirt with epaulets. The uniforms don't mean much; they just make these guys feel official. Pablo's a good man. He doesn't sleep on the job, he's friendly, and he keeps people away from my business. I like that."

The server emerged from the kitchen carrying two steaming plates of food. She placed one in front of

MJ and the other in front of Ned. On each there was half a chicken covered with a brown sauce, rice with black beans stirred in, and one slice of tomato sitting on top of a single leaf of lettuce. The plate was adorned with what appeared to be a single pink rose. Upon closer inspection, however, MJ could see that it was a carved and dyed vegetable. She picked it up and examined it more closely, trying to figure out what the artist had used.

"It's potato," Ned said. "The cooks are really cute about cutting potatoes into all kinds of shapes and things. They cut them out and soak them in cold water and dye to get the color they want."

"That's pretty cool," she offered.

"The brown sauce on your chicken is called mole. (He pronounced it mole-lay.) You'd be surprised at the ingredients. I think you'll like it. I haven't found anyone yet who doesn't."

MJ cut into her chicken and put a small piece into her mouth. She researched the flavor and moaned her approval.

"The Mexicans don't really understand the concept of salad very well," he said. You're lucky if you get a piece of lettuce and slice of tomato with your meal. You're really lucky if they throw on a slice of cucumber, as well. They prefer their vegetables cooked into stews, sauces, or side dishes. When I do make it to the States, the first thing I do is to go somewhere and order a huge Caesar salad. It's probably the one thing that I miss the most down here."

"About this job. Just what will we be doing?" MJ asked.

"A lot of flying, hopefully," Ned answered, as he took another sip of wine. "When things go smoothly, we jump from place to place. We pick up in some places and deliver to other places. Sometimes, we do both. The government has begun to clamp down on the disposal of medical waste, so we have begun to collect it from the stations we visit and drop it off at designated sites. In a sense, we've become garbage men." He looked up from his plate at MJ. "I guess I had better change that to garbage-people, or, at best, sanitary engineers."

MJ laughed and wiped her chin with her napkin. "Oh great! I've traveled thousands of miles and spent thousands of dollars to be a trash collector. My flight instructors will be so proud of me."

"How many of them get to fly DC-3s?" he asked.

"None that I know of," she answered. "Will we have time to give me a little training before we head off to parts unknown?"

"Not really. I figure it's going to be on-the-job-training for you," he answered. "Look at it this way: I can handle that aircraft by myself, so you'll have plenty of time to learn the systems and the copilot stuff. If we get into some kind of trouble, there isn't going to be a whole lot for you to do anyway, except maybe read the emergency checklists. Once you get comfortable with her and have flown her from the right seat for awhile, I'll move you over to the left seat and let you do all the flying. Heaven knows I've got more time in that thing than anyone could ever desire. She's big, but she's just an airplane. I bet you'll feel right at home after just a couple of hours."

MJ thought about what he had said and remembered visiting a field in Oshkosh, Wisconsin, where there were a number of DC-3s being overhauled. After identifying herself as a pilot, the owner gave her a tour of the facilities and took her aboard one of the Gooneys to show her the cockpit. The first thing that impressed her was how high up they were. The owner told her they were seventeen feet up with the tail on the ground. "When level," he said, "it's only fifteen feet off the ground." That seemed substantial to MJ. Everything looked big: the engines, the control wheel and column, the trim wheel, the throttle and prop levers, yet the windows seemed disproportionately small. It was like looking out a ship's porthole. The saving grace was that the side windows slid open and shut easily and gave the pilot a good view of the engine, wing, and

47

ground. MJ pictured herself learning how to fly the big plane, flying over unfamiliar territory in unfamiliar skies. She was confident she could do it, but she also knew that there were going to be some very tense moments along the way.

"Besides picking up the garbage, just what, exactly, do you do, Mr. Greenlawn?" MJ inquired.

"Call me Ned. If I'm to call you MJ, and we're going to be working together for the better part of a year, you might as well start calling me Ned now."

"Fair enough," she agreed. "Can you give me some background about this operation?"

"Sure," he said. "How far back would you like me to go?"

"Well, I don't want to be too nosy, but I guess the more you feel like telling me, the quicker I'll get to know you. Although, there is the argument that if you spoon feed me a little at a time over the next year, we won't lack for conversation."

"Point taken," he said. "I'll try not to bore you with too much too soon."

Ned picked up the wine bottle and refilled both their glasses, gathering his thoughts as he did. He didn't know very much about MJ, either, other than she came recommended by a former close friend of his. She loved to fly and was willing to work for room and board while building flight time toward a career. He decided he would have to go back far enough so she could understand why he was doing what he was doing and doing it in Mexico and Central America.

The colorfully dressed server appeared from the archway through which MJ had first entered the courtyard. She led a man and a woman to one of the tables on the far side. She placed menus in front of each of them, asked them if they would care for something to drink, and drifted past Ned and MJ's table toward the kitchen.

"Is everything OK? Can I get anything for you?" she asked.

"No, gracias, Mariana. Not now. Everything is super bien!" he said, as he raised two fingers to his lips and made a kissing sound.

Mariana smiled at both of them and continued toward the kitchen.

"Mariana is one of the people I brought to Mexico City," Ned offered as a start to his background. "She was living with one of the missionary women in a village not far from Oaxaca, helping whenever she could. They were together for a number of years before the woman returned to the United States. As much as she wanted to adopt Mariana and take her back with her, she just couldn't get through the paperwork and bureaucracy the Mexican government put in her way. She was devastated. Mariana couldn't understand why this woman couldn't just stay in Mexico with her, but the woman had to get back to take care of her mother, who had fallen ill with a terminal form of cancer. It didn't work out for either one of them. I try not to get too attached to the people in these remote areas, but I just felt that I needed to do

something in this case. I felt bad
for both of them. I was friendly
with this couple in Mexico City, so
I made a point of talking to them
about Mariana. They had been trying
to have children of their own for
many years without success. They had
already started to talk to an agency
about adopting a small child when I
told them about Mariana and what
happened. These people were amazing.
They didn't hesitate for an instant.
They said, 'Bring her to us. We'll
work out the details later.' I
thought it was very brave of them,
knowing the mountain of paperwork
they would face, but I was very
happy that Mariana would have a
permanent home. At first she was not
sure, and she was scared. I assured
her that everything was going to be
all right and she would love Mexico
City. That was ten years ago. I stop
to see her and the family when I'm
in the city, and I bring her things
from Oaxaca so she won't forget
where she came from. She has done
very well. She married; she has this
job; she has two beautiful children
of her own, one boy and one girl.
She's one of the lucky ones. It
worked out for her."

Mariana returned to the table and cleared their plates.

"Postre?" she asked.

"Would you like some dessert? I recommend the flan and some coffee."

"I don't know. I'm pretty full."

"I don't know how to tell you this, MJ; this is probably the last good meal in a restaurant you're going to have for quite some time. The rest of this trip will be like camping out. You'll be eating when you can, what you can, and extremely grateful when you get the opportunity to cook something over a campfire instead of eating something cold out of a can. Trust me. Get dessert."

"That's a very convincing argument. OK. I'll go with the flan and coffee."

"Dos," he said to Mariana. She glided back to the kitchen to fill their order.

"That's an interesting story about Mariana, but it didn't tell me much about how you got here, Ned."

"You're right. I guess I had better start with Vietnam."

Mariana returned carrying a tray with the two coffees and flan. She placed a caramelized custard and coffee in front of MJ, along with a small pitcher of cream.

After serving Ned, she asked, "Anything else?"

"No, gracias Mariana. How are Pablito and Maria?"

"They are fine. They are growing so fast I can hardly keep up with them. All they want to do is eat."

"That's probably due to your good cooking. When are you going to take over the kitchen here?" he chided.

"I do enough cooking for my husband and my kids. I don't want to come here and spend my time cooking some more. This is my rest time. I just bring the food and take away the dirty dishes. I don't even have

53

to wash them. No, gracias. I don't want to cook here, Señor."

"It sounds like you have it all figured out, Mariana. Good for you."

She moved away from the table and left them to their conversation. The two in the corner had received their meals and were quietly eating, enjoying the near solitude of the torch-lit courtyard. The peace was enhanced by the meditative sound of the dribbling water in the fountain. MJ was amazed at how effectively the surrounding buildings blocked the noise from the street and made the courtyard an oasis of tranquillity.

Ned glanced at the couple in the corner, took a bite of his dessert, and washed it down with a little coffee. He removed the napkin from his lap, wiped his lips, placed it back onto his lap, rested his forearms on the table, and began his story.

SIX

"Vietnam. Man, what a trip," he
began. "I didn't know what to do
about it. I agreed with Mohammed
Ali; I didn't have anything against
those little brown people, either.
Many of my friends were really gung-
ho and really believed that
Communism was going to spread all
over Asia unless we stopped it in
Vietnam. Like every other kid on the
block, I was impressionable, too,
but I couldn't see how a civil war
in that tiny little country was
going to determine the politics for
the rest of the world. I thought
about going to Canada, but I didn't

55

want to hide for the rest of my life. I thought about becoming a conscientious objector, too, but I really didn't believe that I was. How was I going to convince anyone else that I was if I didn't believe it myself? One night, having exhausted all my other options, I had a long talk with my father. I told him I was really scared. I told him that in no way did I want to kill anyone, anywhere, at any time. He was a doctor, and he told me he knew what I was feeling. He asked me if I would serve in the armed forces as long as I didn't have to take a combative role. I hadn't thought about that, but it was a no-brainer. 'Sure,' I said. But, how am I going to do that? I didn't have a clue as to what the military was all about. I thought everyone who was in the Army or Marines carried weapons and was taught to kill people. I thought the Air Force people flew planes, or fixed them, and the Navy people sailed boats. What did I know? Dad made a few phone calls and found that if I enlisted, they would guarantee me the job of my choice. He explained to the people he spoke with that I wouldn't take up weapons against anyone, but I was willing to serve; they suggested I sign up for the Army medical corps and become a corpsman. They told him that the Army won't guarantee anything, but they needed corpsmen. It was even possible that I wouldn't have to go to Vietnam; I might be assigned to a hospital here in the States or somewhere else overseas. Corpsmen were needed in every unit, whether they were in a combat situation or not. It looked like my best option, and Dad agreed. He said that whatever I did was OK with him. He wasn't too keen on the war either."

"So, you were like a medic?" MJ asked.

"That's exactly what I was. And you can forget about some plush job in a hospital in the States or Europe or Japan or Okinawa. They put me with a unit on its way to Vietnam the moment I finished my training. You want to talk about on-the-job-training? I was scared to death, as was just about everyone else around me. I didn't even have time to get broken-in with some minor stuff, like cuts and scratches or foot problems or whatever. After one week of in-country orientation, they

57

shipped us up north to an area where there was some of the heaviest fighting in the country. I was stationed at a firebase. It's kind of like a permanent spot where they have artillery and mortars and fire them for support of the troops that are out in the bush hunting the enemy. The only problem was that we were pretty exposed. Most of these firebases were on a hill, and the North Vietnamese targeted us on a regular basis. We were dug in pretty well, but we still took casualties. That was my introduction to being a corpsman in the field. I learned to dress more kinds of wounds in more kinds of places than I thought was possible. During a firefight, or a barrage, I would be running from body to body for hours on end. Sometimes I thought it was never going to stop. When it finally did, I would go into my bunker and just crash. No food. No water. Just sleep. That's all I wanted. I lost a lot of weight."

MJ thought from the looks of him it didn't seem as if he ever got it back, either.

"About three months into my first tour . . . " he started.

"First tour?" she interrupted.

"Yes, my first tour. There were three."

"Three tours in Vietnam?" she asked incredulously. "Didn't each tour last a year?"

"You got it," he said. "In all the other wars this country has been involved in, nobody came home unless they were wounded, dead, or the war had ended. Someone got the bright idea that this war could be fought better if we only kept our people there for a year and then let them come home. Unless, of course, they signed up for another tour, as I did."

"Why on earth would you sign up for another tour if you didn't want to be there in the first place?"

"Well, I'm not sure you'll understand it, but I got comfortable. Maybe independent is a better word," he tossed out before she had a chance to respond.

"You're right," she said. "I don't understand." She pushed her dessert plate aside, put both elbows on the table, folded her hands, and rested her chin on them. "Go on."

"You get numb when you're dealing with death and destruction all the time," he continued. "I mean, don't get me wrong, I felt for those guys all shot-up and bleeding. You couldn't let it get to you, or you'd be paralyzed. You wouldn't get anything done. It's the same with fear; I was scared to death that I was going to be the next one to be ripped apart by shrapnel or take a bullet or step on a landmine or whatever. However, it didn't happen, at least during the first couple of years. I got tired of being afraid, just worn out from it, I guess. So, I stopped thinking about it and just did my job. I got very good at it, I must say. My company commander noticed how efficient I had become, so he promoted me and assigned me to a reconnaissance squad. Sometimes they were ambushed, and this company commander had it in his head that he wasn't going to allow a single one of his men to be left behind, especially in the bush. So he put me with them and told me to make sure that everyone got back. It was a pretty tall order, but I liked the idea of being with a smaller group and not being so overworked that I was tired all the time. Besides, I didn't have any choice in the matter. Making the best of a bad situation, I thought. Are you bored, yet?" he asked.

"No, not at all. But, I do have to go to the bathroom. It's probably the wine limiting my seat time. Will you excuse me, please?"

"Absolutely," he said. "Actually, that's not a bad idea. I'll meet you back here. The ladies room is through that archway you came in and past the stairs. It's on the left."

"Thanks. I'll be right back."

Ned and MJ both got up at the same time and headed out of the courtyard under the watchful eyes of the couple in the corner, who were now enjoying their coffee and smoking cigarettes. The smoke rose gently through the hanging plants, caught the updraft from the burning

61

torches, and disappeared into the warm Mexican evening.

Ned stopped briefly to talk to Mariana, who was standing just outside the kitchen doors. He told her they would be right back and to please fill the cups with fresh coffee. He also requested some bottled water for both of them, just in case MJ had her fill of coffee but needed something to quench her thirst. Mariana smiled and gently slapped him on the arm for something he said to kid her, no doubt, as he walked away. She was obviously fond of him.

The coffee and water were on the table when MJ returned. Ned had arrived first and was stirring his coffee slowly. His head was down; he seemed to be mesmerized by the motion of the spoon going around and around in the cup. When MJ sat down, he stopped and removed the spoon from the cup, placing it on the saucer. He lifted the cup from the saucer, took a couple of short sips, and put it down. Mary Jane did the same and gave him her undivided attention.

"More?" he asked.

"Sure," she answered. "I don't have anywhere to go and it's interesting. I still want to know why you signed up for additional tours."

"It's probably hard for someone else to understand. Sometimes it's a little overwhelming for me, too, but something happened, spending all that time in the bush. I began to like it. Not the firefights and mines and booby-traps, don't get me wrong. I was learning how to take care of myself as well as help other people. It was a confidence-builder being out there. It was beautiful. It's a beautiful country, Vietnam. You don't hear much about that, or at least you didn't then. I think I fell in love with the jungle, the mountains, and clear rivers and streams. I also didn't have to put up with so much of the bullshit that was always a part of being at a base camp, like people yelling at me, telling me what to do: clean this, pick up that, tuck in that shirt, blouse those boots, Soldier. There was none of that chicken-shit stuff. It was just us and occasionally the enemy, of course. Usually, those were brief moments: contact, a lot of gunfire from both sides, and then quiet. We pull back; they disappear into the jungle. We call in the coordinates; the artillery or mortars do their thing, and then it was quiet again. Most of the time, we didn't find anything. Sometimes, we would stay out for four or five days at a time, zigzagging back and forth across trails, looking for signs that the VC or the regulars had been moving. I learned a lot about living off the land, too. It got so that I liked the food I took from the jungle more than the stuff the Army had us carry. Eating off the land, I didn't have to haul the garbage back to camp. I became a regular jungle rat."

"So your love of the jungle is what kept you going back?"

"I guess I'd have to say, partially, yes. Things didn't sink in until I came home. With only a week left in country, they sent me back to Saigon to process out. I was as excited as the next guy about getting back to the States and warm showers and burgers and all that stuff; I was really looking forward to it. It was great, too, when I did get home. I loved seeing everybody and getting back into my old room and cruising the old haunts. I also saw the war from the same perspective that most people in the US were seeing it . . . the TV. Between that, the papers, and all the news about the demonstrators, man, I wondered if we were talking about the same war. People were asking me all kinds of questions, but mostly they wanted to know if I had killed anyone. Even after I told them that I was a medic, they still wanted all the gory details of what it was like to kill someone. If it wasn't that, they wanted to know why I would ever think about participating in an immoral war. I began to feel as though I didn't belong in my own hometown anymore, and I missed the bush. I mean, after you spend the better part of a year walking mountain trails, the city can really grate on your senses. I had a constant headache from all the noise that most people just take for granted. Finally, I had enough. I knew that I couldn't stay, and I knew that I didn't know how to do much of anything except be a medic.

So I went back to the recruiting office and asked about going back. I also asked them about being able to work in the field and if they could guarantee that. The sergeant told me that the only way they could guarantee a slot back in the field was for me to train with the Green Berets. He said that most of them were still operating as advisors and spent most of their time in the mountains, recruiting the local indigenous tribes and training them to help in the war effort. I told him that I wouldn't fight. He looked at me kind of funny, but then he told me that they needed corpsmen, too, and that I would probably be used to set up and operate clinics to help the locals. I didn't like the idea of having to train to be a Green Beret; I saw them as elite assassins. However, I did like the idea of getting to know the natives and helping them live a better life. I guess I was still idealistic at that stage of the game. I signed on the dotted line, and they sent me off to become a Green Beret. My dad was not happy with me, but at that point I really didn't care. I was not the same person I was when I first went. Unfortunately, he didn't have a chance to get to know the new me. The physical training was a bear, even if I was in good shape from my first year in country. The good news came when we began survival training. I had the advantage of already having been in Vietnam and living off the land, so the drill sergeants had me do most of the training for them. I felt important. I was back in the jungle before I knew it."

"Didn't your dad try to stop you?"

"He didn't want me to go back. He said that I had done my share and that I didn't owe the country anything more. I told him that I wasn't doing this for the country; I was doing it for me. I tried to explain to him how much I loved the bush, and he understood that. What he couldn't understand was why I needed to go to Vietnam to spend time in the wild. Why couldn't I just go to Montana or Colorado or somewhere else with mountains and woods? I really didn't have an answer for him; I just wanted to be back in the bush in Vietnam. Maybe I needed the adrenaline rush from the potential danger inherent in a country at war. Who knows? I told him that this time I would be working with the locals in the mountains and that I would have a chance to help them by setting up clinics, giving vaccinations, and teaching them about sanitation and nutrition. He just kept asking, 'Vietnam? Why Vietnam?' We couldn't come to an understanding. I shipped out without saying goodbye. I've always regretted that; he died of a heart attack during my third tour. The Army was willing to let me go home for the funeral, but I didn't see the point. I remember him for who he was and what he did for me. I didn't need to see him laid-out in a coffin. I called my mother to see how she was doing. She was too numb to talk to me."

Ned unscrewed the cap on the bottled water and took a long drink. He had been talking non-stop, and it was still warm, although the sun had set a couple of hours ago.

"I'm sorry about your dad," MJ offered. "It sounds like you had a pretty good relationship with him."

"Yeah. We did OK. I always appreciated him helping me figure out the war thing. I bet he'd be working with me now if he had lived. He liked helping people and he always had to be doing something. That's probably why he had the heart attack. I'd bet he would have never retired if he had reached that age. He liked his work too much."

"So what about those other two tours?" MJ pushed.

"Not much else to tell you. I worked with the Green Berets for both of them; I helped a lot of people in the mountains. I helped many of our guys, too. Being so far away from a constant source of medical supplies, and not having a doctor on our team, I learned how to do some incredible things. I bet I could show a fully licensed doctor a thing or two. The great thing about working in the field was that I also learned a lot about herbal medicine. People who live so close to the land have an intimate knowledge of the vegetation and what it's good for. I've seen some incredible healing take place with a wound after the application of a local poultice. I

69

could never have gotten the kind of medical education in the States that I received in Vietnam. Sure, the US Army got me started and gave me the opportunity, but that field experience, and the experience with the natives, was what sewed it up for me."

"That's an incredible story," MJ interjected. "And all that time over there you never got shot?"

"Shot? Sort of. Wounded? Yes," he came back. "When both sides are lobbing artillery and mortars all over the place, and the US is dropping bombs from so high up you can't even see the planes, it was a miracle that everyone didn't take a hit. As for me, I earned a Purple Heart for bomb fragments delivered to Cambodia during the Christmas cease-fire that didn't quite make it to Cambodia; my Christmas present from former President Nixon. We were operating right on the border, so it's not exactly his entire fault. Whatever the reason, the bombs started going off around us before we had a chance to take cover. We lost some good people during that raid . . . some Green Beanies and some indigenous, too. I had picked up a kid who got blown out of his hut and was heading for a trench when a fragment found me."

Ned traced the scar that went from the edge of his eye down his cheek and behind the beard.

"I didn't know I was hit until I dove into the trench and tried to cover the kid with my body. All of a sudden, there was blood all over him. I turned him over and looked for the wound, but I couldn't find anything. Then I reached up and felt my face; it was soaked, and a piece of my cheek was flapping when I rubbed the side of my face. The baby regained consciousness right after that and started crying. The blast must have knocked him out, but it didn't seem to hurt him otherwise. One of the guys ran over to where we were, looked at me, reached down, and took the baby from me. He reached into his pouch, pulled out a field bandage, and handed it to me. I pressed it against the side of my face, making sure that the loose skin was where it should be, and then I went up to the center of the village to find someone to help me

71

stitch it up. Fortunately, the woman who helped me was a magician with a needle. I don't think a plastic surgeon could have done much better."

MJ took another look at the scar. She was sure that a plastic surgeon could have done a better job of it, but she didn't offer that opinion to Ned.

"That's the only wound you had over the entire three year period?" she asked.

"Pretty much. I have a few other small scars here and there, mostly from mortar fragments. They were nuisance wounds more than anything else. I did catch a round through my calf, once. Friendly fire. Some joker was clearing the breech of an M-60 machine gun and failed to catch the chambered round in his hand. It fell into the hot brass near the gun and cooked-off; the hot brass ignited the unexpended bullet. I was working on a guy who was shot twice in the leg when it hit me. It hurt like hell, but I can laugh about it now. They even gave me another Purple Heart!"

"Laugh about it? When you almost get killed by your own men?"

"You know what I mean. It's always such trauma while it's taking place, but you can look back and see the irony of it all: soldier takes two in the leg from enemy fire; medic helps soldier with two in the leg from enemy fire; medic takes one in the leg from friendly fire. Score: enemy-2, friendlies-1. Enemy still ahead." Ned grinned as he took another drink from his bottled water.

MJ didn't laugh. She didn't see any humor in troops getting blasted by their own men. To her, it was just stupid.

"So what happened when you returned to the States for good?" she wanted to know.

"What? You haven't had enough of me already?" Ned said, as he placed the bottle back on the table.

"Not quite," she said. How did you end up down here?"

73

"Well, you remember what I told you about not liking cities, with all their noise and what-all? You remember what I told you about being out in the bush? Well, I found working down here to be about as close to what I had in Vietnam as I could find."

"And the flying part?" she asked. "Nelson told me a little about how you got the license to fly the DC-3, but he didn't say anything about how you got started flying in the first place."

"Not much of a story there, actually," he started. "When I got back to the States, I was discharged from the Army in California. Because I'd done three tours in Vietnam, I didn't owe them any more time; so I was out all the way. No reserve time was necessary. I had some money socked away and the GI Bill money if I wanted it. I was pretty well set. I drifted up the coast to northern California, hit Eureka, and turned east. I got as far as the mountains and decided to hang out there for a while. One day while not doing anything in particular, I heard an airplane overhead. I watched as he circled down and then disappeared behind a ridge. I walked over that ridge and saw that he had landed at a small airport that was snuggled between some rolling hills and Ponderosa pines. As I said, I didn't have anything better to do, so I walked down the hill and over to the first building I came to on the field. There was a guy out front putting fuel in this little, yellow tail-dragger. A Super Cub he called it. We began talking, and he told me that he, too, had been to Vietnam back in the sixties. We hit it off right away. Anyway, he asked me if I'd ever been up in a small plane before, and I told him no. The next thing I knew I was strapped into the back seat of that thing and we were soaring over the hills and through the valleys of northern California. It was great! We talked some more when we got back on the ground, and I found out that he ran a small flight training operation. He told me that if I wanted to learn to fly, I could use my GI benefits to pay for it. The rest is history, as they say."

MJ opened her bottle of water and poured some of it into her empty coffee cup. She took a couple of sips and looked back up at Ned.

"OK. That explains how you got started in aviation. How did you end up in Mexico?" she asked.

"Missionaries."

MJ raised an eyebrow and looked at him, puzzled.

"Missionaries," he repeated. While I was finishing up my flight training with Ernie—I don't think I mentioned his name earlier—he introduced me to some friends of his who spent a lot of time doing missionary work in Central America. They were joking about how much time they spent driving from one place to another when Ernie suggested they take me along with them and *fly* to their remote outposts. We all laughed . . . at first. A few weeks later these people came back to me and asked if I would be willing to fly for them. I didn't have anything better to do, so I said sure. Ernie helped them find a plane and checked me out in it. It was a Cessna 182, a small, high wing four-seater with a good bit of power. Nothing fancy.

Next thing I knew I was flying all over Central America and Mexico. It was great experience. Most of the time we just went from dirt strip to grass strip to practically no strip. I became a full-blown bush pilot and learned those countries from treetop to mountaintop and sea to shining sea. Actually, that's how I met Nelson, too."

"Really? Well, I guess that would make sense. He did spend a lot of time down here. It was probably inevitable that you would run into one another."

"More like lucky . . . for him," he said.

"How so?"

"Nelson had taken a tumble and broken his leg while in some God-awful, way out-of-the-way place in Guatemala. The climate in those places is perfect for producing infections, even from the simplest of wounds. Nelson had a compound-complex fracture; the bone tore right through the skin. It was going to be a long haul to get him to a doctor, and everyone was sure that he would lose the leg to gangrene before they got him out. We just happened by a couple of days after the accident and were able to fly him out to Guatemala City, where he got the help he needed to save the leg. Things were a little slow for us at the time, so I stayed with him to keep him company and cheer him up. We got to know each other pretty well, and I saw him numerous times after that. He's one of the few people I still keep in touch with after all these years and all the people I've met down here. He's a nice guy. I like him."

"Yes. I like him too. He's always been really friendly and helpful to my family and me. I'm not much of a church person, but I've always enjoyed helping Nelson with special projects and outings. I've even taken him up in the plane a couple of times. He says he enjoys it, but I always see that sigh of relief when we touch down. Some people are just not meant for flying, I guess."

"Ain't that the truth. I believe I have tested the faith of many a missionary in the last twenty-plus years," Ned added. "Probably strengthened a few of them and converted a few. I have to admit, whether they like flying or not, they would fly with me to get to those outposts. They put their faith in God, prayed for me every step of the way, and did what they felt they were called to do. You've got to admire them."

"Speaking of flying," MJ chimed in. Don't we have to get up pretty early in the morning?"

"Mmmm. 11:30," he said, looking down at his watch. "Where does the time go? I guess we had better call it a night. We'll have plenty of time to continue this conversation later."

"I want to thank you for giving me this opportunity, Ned, and for dinner and telling me about your experiences. It's been fascinating."

"I talk too much, but you're welcome, MJ. You're a good listener. I hope I didn't bore you to death. Before you thank me for bringing you on board, you had better wait a few weeks. You might not feel the same way by then."

"I'll take my chances," she said. "And, no, you didn't bore me. You're one of the most interesting people I've ever met. Besides, where else am I going to get the chance to fly a Gooney Bird? Certainly not with the good ol' boys up north."

Ned hung on the last statement and hesitated a bit before responding.

"She's a beautiful bird, MJ. She'll treat you right if you take care of her. By the time you finish the year with her, you'll think she's either adopted you as her little sister or plotted to see that you never fly another. It's a funny thing that way."

MJ didn't understand his comment. All she knew was that she was going to be flying a beautiful airplane. That was enough for her. She pushed her chair back from the table, stood up, and stretched. Ned got up, too, and went over to Mariana, who was standing patiently near the kitchen doors. He reached into his pocket and took out a wad of bills, peeled off several, and gave them to her. He put the rest back into his pocket and returned to the table.

"Sorry I kept you up so long, MJ. Four-in-the-morning is going to come around pretty quickly."

"No problem. I'm so excited, I probably won't sleep."

"I understand, but try and get some rest," he said. We have quite a lot to do tomorrow, and we *will* be flying."

They walked out to the front desk. Ned said something in Spanish to the clerk on duty, smiled, and turned to MJ.

"It's been an enjoyable evening, MJ," he said, as he offered her his hand. "I'm looking forward to working with you. I appreciate your willingness to come down here and work for no pay under some pretty harsh working conditions to boot. I hope you don't regret it."

"Not a chance," she said. "I wouldn't miss this for anything. See you in the morning."

81

"Goodnight, MJ," he said, as he turned and walked down the hall to the front entrance. "Make sure you lock your door."

Ned's last comment brought MJ back to the reality of her situation. She was alone in a large foreign city for the first time. The pleasantness of the evening in the quiet courtyard had wiped away the anxiety she felt after the chaotic ride through this bustling city. She would definitely be locking her door behind her. Now she wondered, even more so, if she would be getting any sleep at all.

SEVEN

The ride from Mexico City to the airstrip took a little more than an hour-and-a-half. Rodrigo showed up at the hotel on time and helped her with her things, which she had placed in front of the hotel desk moments before he arrived. He brought her some hot coffee and Mexican pastries, for which she was extremely grateful. The meal from the previous evening was filling, but MJ had a hard time getting going in the morning until she had her first cup of coffee and something to eat.

Ned had all the supplies loaded onto the truck by the time she arrived at the warehouse. MJ bid farewell to Rodrigo, slipped him a few pesos for his fine service, and climbed into the cab of the truck with Ned. They were out of the city and climbing into the surrounding hills by the time the sun began to light the landscape. MJ took in the beautiful vistas of the mountain pass and then the expansive valley below, as the truck bounced along the thruway and onward toward their destination.

MJ thought she should be feeling worse than she did with so little sleep behind her. She figured the adrenaline from the initial excitement was still holding her up. She had flown tired before, but now she was having second thoughts about getting her first taste of the Gooney Bird with so little sleep under her belt.

"There she is," Ned said, as they pulled off the dirt road toward the big DC-3. "Isn't she the most beautiful ugly thing you ever saw?"

"She certainly is big. I don't know about the ugly part, though."

"She won't seem so intimidating after you've flown her for a while."

"Easy for you to say."

Ned pulled the truck up to the plane and backed it up to the cargo door. Antonio, Ned's only employee and guard, had the cargo doors open and was waiting for them.

"Buenos días, Antonio," Ned said, as he came around to the back of the truck and opened the door. "How are you doing this fine morning?"

"Fine, Señor," Antonio answered. "And you?"

"Not bad, Antonio, not bad. I'd like you to meet Mary Jane Carlson, my new copilot," Ned said, as MJ appeared at the back of the truck.

The surprise on Antonio's face was more than obvious. Evidently Ned hadn't told him that his new copilot was a woman.

"Buenos días, Señorita," he offered politely. "Are you really going to fly this plane with Señor Ned?" he asked.

"Yes, I'm really going to fly this plane with Ned," she answered. "It's nice to meet you, Antonio. Are you going to be coming with us?"

"Me?" he said. "No, Señorita. No way! You won't ever see me in this plane unless it's on the ground. This plane is very old; can't you see? I won't fly in a new plane, so there is no way I'm going to fly in this one. Maybe you are as crazy as Señor Ned, but me, I want to live a very long time."

"Antonio," asked Ned. "How long have I been flying this plane?"

"Many years, I guess," answered Antonio.

"Very many years, Antonio. Have I ever crashed this plane?"

"No, Señor. But, it only takes one time. No?"

"No. I can put this bird down anywhere and walk away without a scratch. She's made to fly, Antonio. She loves to fly. Don't you, Big Girl," he said, as he slapped the fuselage with a gloved hand.

"Well, you two can do all the flying you want. I'll be here waiting for you, and I'll take good care of your airplane for you. But I'm not going inside that thing and leave the ground. Never! Have you been flying very long, Marijuana?" Antonio asked.

"Marijuana?" MJ repeated.

"That's your name in Spanish, MJ," Ned answered. I suggest you avoid the Spanish version, especially at the major airports."

"Fine with me. I've been flying for about six years on my own, Antonio. Before that, I flew with my father; he started me when I was ten. I've spent a lot of time in the air."

"Mmmm. Your father is a brave man. I think that you are the first lady pilot that I ever see. Of course, out here, I don't see many pilots anyway—just Señor Ned."

"There aren't too many of us, compared to the number of men flying," she said, "Our numbers are growing, though."

"I bet there aren't any lady pilots in Mexico," Antonio said. "Of course, if there were, I wouldn't know it. This is the only place I know. In fact, this is the only airplane that I know."

"Well, now you can say that you know a lady pilot, Antonio," she said. "It's nice to meet you."

MJ, Ned, and Antonio unloaded the truck into the DC-3 and secured the load.

"Is there anything else you need, Señor Ned?" he asked.

"No, thanks. We should be back in about a week. If you get the chance, change the oil in the truck and give it a good bath. It has gotten pretty grungy from all the dust in the city and the ride down here."

Ned pulled a wad of pesos from his pocket, peeled off a few, and gave them to Antonio.

"OK, no problem. It will be very clean when you get back."

"Thanks. See you next week," Ned said.

Antonio climbed into the truck and started it. He pulled slowly away from the plane and drove back toward the highway and Tepotzlan, where he lived.

"Well, MJ, shall we get started?" Ned asked.

"That's what I'm here for. Where do we begin?"

"Just like any other flight, MJ, with the pre-flight."

Ned walked up to the cockpit and returned with the checklist for the plane.

"C'mon," he said. "We'll start outside."

Ned went through the checklist with MJ, having her do all the necessary checks while he read them off the list. Once completed, they climbed into the aircraft, secured the door, and buckled themselves in. Ned continued to read the list and point out the various buttons, dials, and switches, most of which were very familiar to MJ. However, like learning any new airplane, she had to get used to where everything was located. Since it was her first time in this bird, Ned did the startup routine and demonstrated the procedure. In a matter of minutes, the big radial engines of the DC-3 had come alive and were idling smoothly.

"We're not going that far today, MJ. I thought I'd make your introductory flight a relatively short one, so that we can take some time to go over basic maneuvers and give you a chance to get a feel for the plane."

"Fine with me. I just hope I don't fall asleep in the middle of it."

"I doubt you will. I'll keep you busy so you don't get bored."

"I bet. Where are we going?"

"To a little strip between Oaxaca and Puerto Escondido. Not too far from the beach, actually," he answered. "OK, MJ. I've released the parking brake and the tail wheel. Let's taxi down there to the right. We'll do our run-up there. Just ease the throttles forward and then retard them once she gets around the corner and rolling."

MJ advanced the throttles slowly until the plane began to move. She pulled the throttle on the right engine, allowing the power of the left engine to pull them around the turn, at the same time applying full right rudder and just a light tap on the right brake. The brake squealed in protest and grabbed quickly, bringing the big plane around quicker than MJ anticipated. She had to hit full left rudder and jockey the throttles to straighten the plane's path.

"Taxiing this thing is probably the hardest thing you'll have to do, MJ. Everyone has a hard time at first. The brakes are probably a

91

little more sensitive than usual due to lack of use this past week."

"Man, my legs really feel the workout on these peddles," she said.

Ned laughed. "You'll be able to run a marathon by the end of the year, MJ. It's good for you."

"Maybe it is," she agreed, "but right now, this is a lot of work!"

At the end of the field, Ned had MJ spin the plane around toward the departing end of the grass strip. He went back to the checklist and tutored MJ through the pre-takeoff items. Once completed, he released the parking brake and locked the tail wheel.

"OK, MJ, if anything goes wrong up to V1/V2, our rotation point, we will abort the takeoff. After that, it becomes an in-flight emergency. I'll take over and you just sit tight. Later on, when you know the plane better, we can divide the chores. I may call for the emergency checklist if we have time and opportunity, but I'll probably just get this thing back around and on the ground as quickly as possible. Now, advance the throttles steadily until I tap the back of your hand. Good! Keep your hand lightly on the throttles while I set the manifold pressure; we'll use forty-five inches. OK, airspeed is sixty. Push on the yoke and get the tail off the ground. Good. Here comes V2, eighty-five knots. Rotate."

MJ pulled back on the yoke and the DC-3 floated off the field like a feather in a breeze.

"Now," he continued, let the plane accelerate to about 105. We're out of runway, gear up." Ned reached down, unlatched the safety ring and pulled up on the gear-locking lever. He then reached over and pulled the gear lever out and up. "So far, so good," he said. "Here's your trim wheel. Give it a slight twist and she'll do this all by herself."

MJ trimmed the nose slightly down until the airspeed settled on 105 knots. Ned placed the gear handle in neutral and pointed out the gear-unsafe amber light in front of MJ on the panel. He also showed her the gear-down pressure gauge that now read zero.

"How high?" MJ asked.

"Let's take her to 4500 feet. Time for METO—that's our maximum except for take-off power. I'll set that for you. Another five-hundred feet and I'll set your climb power."

"She really is smooth," MJ commented.

"Oh she's smooth all right," he said. "Like I told you, she's a big bird; but once you get used to that she's just another airplane. You've got a lot of wing working for you and 1200 horses a side if you need them. She's a joy to fly."

Ned set the climb power as they climbed through one thousand feet above ground level, checked to make sure the cowl flaps were in the "trail" position, and turned off the electric fuel pumps one at a time.

"We're flying!" he said, as he looked over to MJ with a big grin.

"I think I'm going to like this," she came back. "A lot!"

"I bet you will. At least the flying part," he said. "Take about a one-fifty degree heading, for now."

MJ worked the rudder and column in unison to turn the DC-3 to the requested heading and bumped the power up an inch as they climbed through another thousand feet.

"Man, it's like turning a tank," she said, wrestling with the large wheel on the column.

"It takes a little extra effort. Like your legs, your arms will get accustomed, too. It just takes time."

MJ eased the nose forward as they approached their desired altitude and trimmed it down. Once they reached their cruising speed of 140 knots, Ned had her reduce the throttles to twenty-eight inches of manifold pressure and adjust the propeller rpm to the proper cruise setting. He looked at his watch and said, "We'll give her about five minutes before we set the mixtures to auto-lean. It usually takes that long for the engine temps to stabilize."

"This thing has auto-lean?" she asked.

"You bet. Works great, too . . . usually. Like anything in flying, you don't trust it. You constantly check and crosscheck everything. All it takes is one screw-up to ruin your whole day."

When they were about halfway to their destination and Ned felt that MJ was feeling comfortable with the plane, he told her that it was time for some basic maneuvers. He wanted her to experience a few of the essentials early on.

"OK, MJ. Let's slow her down to about 110-115 knots and re-trim. The first thing we're going to do is some steep turns. I'll start you off easy."

"Thanks. Don't scare me too soon. I just got here."

"No problem," he assured her. "Just crank her over to about forty to forty-five degrees. Watch how fast the airspeed is affected."

MJ flew the plane 360 degrees back to their starting point.

"That didn't feel too bad," she said. "It does eat up some airspeed, though."

"Yes it does," he said. "Remember that when you're coming in low and slow. Don't over bank!"

"Roger that," she said.

"Let's slow her down some more and stall her clean," he said.

"Stall her! You're going to deliberately stall this big thing?" she asked.

"Not me. You! I've got the power back. Just keep trimming her up and keep an eye on your airspeed. See if you can feel the buffet.

MJ slowed the plane until it was just above the indicated airspeed where the plane should stall in a clean configuration.

"A little more," he said.

MJ pulled back a bit more on the column. The big plane began to groan and shudder and then suddenly dipped sharply to the left.

"Right rudder, level the wings, nose down," he ordered, calmly and smoothly. "Good. Level her off and ease the nose up for climb. Now bring your props and power back to climb configuration. OK, great! Let's go up and do it again!" he said, like a kid who just slid down a giant slide and was headed up the ladder to do it again.

"Whoa!" MJ breathed. "Man, it went over pretty quickly."

"It can. She doesn't always, but she can. I've had some new copilots take her right over onto her back. Now *that's* exciting," he said.

"I bet."

"This time, we're going to dirty her up before stalling her. You recover just like any other stall recovery from the landing configuration. You want to get the flaps up quickly; they produce a lot of drag. Just call for flaps first, and then wait until you have a positive rate of climb before you call for the gear," he explained.

MJ slowed the plane as Ned put the flaps down in increments and lowered the gear. MJ reduced the power and trimmed the nose, as before. The big Gooney slowed and shuddered, but didn't groan this time before it stalled. Both wings stalled at the same time and the nose of the big bird fell toward the earth. MJ called for flaps one-quarter, pushed the prop and throttle levers to the climb setting, lifted the nose to level flight, and then eased the plane to a positive climb attitude. She established a positive rate of climb, called for gear up, and then the rest of the flaps up. The plane climbed easily to altitude, where MJ trimmed her and set the power and props for cruise.

"Piece of cake, eh, MJ?" Ned asked.

"A little easier than I expected," she answered. "However, I would just

Rick Byam

as soon avoid the possibility of stalling this thing all together."

"Anything is possible, MJ," he said. "It's the probabilities you need to keep under control."

MJ looked down on the landscape flowing under the DC-3 as they made their way south. She could see the coast to her right and mountains to the left and more mountainous terrain in front of them. This was a big country, and it was beautiful, too. MJ was not sorry she made the decision to come here and fly with Ned.

"Drop her down to two thousand, MJ. Just leave the throttles where they are, put the mixtures into auto-rich, and trim the nose to a five-degree down pitch."

MJ followed his instructions, and the plane began a slow descent toward their destination.

"Swing out more toward the coast. We usually have a sea breeze blowing in over the strip, so we'll plan on a downwind entry for this landing," he instructed.

MJ maneuvered the "Doug" out toward the coast and leveled off at two thousand feet. Ned reached up and flipped on the boost pumps, made sure that the tail wheel was locked, tested the hydraulic system by stepping on the brakes and releasing them, and flipped on the landing lights.

"Why the landing lights way out here, Ned?"

"They have no radio, so there's no way they know that we're coming, other than the fact that we usually show up about this time. I usually put the landing lights on and make a pass over the field to alert them. Otherwise, I might surprise someone playing on the strip or grazing cattle or something. It's better to be safe than sorry. There it is."

MJ looked out in front of the plane and saw nothing but jungle.

"Where?" she asked. "I don't see anything but trees."

"You will. Be patient," he said. "I've been here so many times that I know exactly where it is by a million different landmarks. You will, too, after a few trips. Bring her down to fifteen hundred and power back to twenty inches."

MJ did as she was instructed. When she dropped the nose to continue the descent, she caught sight of a small clearing that quickly passed underneath the fuselage of the plane.

"Was that it?" she asked.

"That was it," he confirmed. "Hang a right and maintain fifteen hundred. I'm giving you one-quarter flaps and dropping the gear. Keep trimming to maintain altitude. This will slow you to about 100 knots."

MJ trimmed the airplane and watched the airspeed diminish. She had no idea where the strip was at this moment; she had to rely on Ned to set her up for a landing.

"OK, MJ. Start her down five hundred feet a minute."

MJ trimmed the nose down until she had the required descent rate.

"Start a shallow bank, about twenty degrees, no more. Here comes flaps one-half," Ned said, as he looked out the window and gauged the landing.

The next level of flaps slowed the plane another ten knots. MJ kept the 500 feet-per-minute descent rate steady.

"Looking good, MJ."

"You want *me* to land here?" she asked.

Ned looked at her and smiled, a twinkle in his eye.

"That's how you learn, Kiddo. That's how you learn. Do you have the field in sight?"

"If it's that little narrow strip and the only place with no trees on it, yes," she answered.

"Good. Here we go. Flaps three-quarters."

When they were about one-quarter mile from the field, Ned lowered the flaps the rest of the way and had MJ hold the airspeed to 85 knots.

"As we cross the end of the field, MJ, work your throttles back and start your flare. As soon as the mains touch down, push forward on the column to keep the wheels planted on the field."

The Gooney passed over the end of the field, slowed, and settled onto the makeshift airstrip.

"Beautiful," he said. "Use your feet, and throttles if necessary, to keep her straight. When we hit sixty knots, pull gently on the column and fly the tail wheel down. We're probably going to have to add a little brake now, too."

The plane slowed almost to a stop. Ned took the controls and spun the plane around, pulled forward a little to lock the tail wheel, and came to a full stop. He shut off the boost pumps, lights, pulled the mixture to idle/cutoff, then reached up and turned off the magnetos, the master switch, the radio master, and, finally, the master battery switch.

Ned unbuckled his seatbelt, walked the slanted fuselage to the cargo doors, and opened them. The hot, steamy air rushed in and filled the plane. There was a hint of salt in the air, no doubt a result of the sea breeze Ned mentioned. He put the small ladder in place and climbed down, carrying the control surface locks and tail wheel chock. MJ followed close behind.

"I can hardly walk my knees are so shaky," she said.

"Happens to everybody at first. A couple of more flights and you'll be fine."

"I hope so. I don't think I'd be very useful loading and unloading with rubber legs like these."

"Well, MJ, in spite of your leg problem, you did a good job. That was a great landing!"

"Thanks," she said. "Not a lot of room for error, is there?"

"Not on these remote strips there isn't. Wait 'til you fly in and out

105

of these places for a month or so, and then go back and land on some hard-surfaced runway. You'll think you're landing on a runway that never ends."

"Sounds like fun," she said. "What now?"

"We're just picking up some medical waste. Garbage collectors, remember?"

"Oh yeah. I forgot."

"We'll be spending the night here, and then it's on to Belize. You'll like it there; they speak English. It's a nice flight, too."

MJ followed Ned toward the jungle and a group of locals colorfully dressed in their native garb. She remembered the camera she left in her pack and started back for it.

"Ned!" she called out. "Will they mind if I get a few pictures?"

"Not at all. I do it all the time."

MJ grabbed the camera and joined Ned, who was talking with a woman dressed in khakis with a stethoscope draped around her neck.

"Doctor, I would like you to meet my new copilot, Mary Jane Carlson—MJ," he said. "MJ, meet Dr. Sylvia Melikian, a pilot herself, no less."

"Hi," MJ said, and shook the doctor's hand. "It's nice to meet another woman pilot so far from home."

"Nice to meet you, MJ," replied the doctor. "You couldn't be flying with a better captain."

"It's obvious that she's never flown with me," Ned said. "Here, MJ, let me get a picture of you and the doctor with some of the people from the village."

Doctor Melikian pulled MJ into the group, and Ned snapped a couple of pictures.

"Where's your plane, Doctor?" MJ asked.

"In Oaxaca," Sylvia answered. "I took it up there for its annual inspection. It should be ready by the end of the week. There's plenty to do here, so I don't mind being without it for a while. Is this your first time south of the border?"

"Yes."

"Like it?"

"Love it."

"It grows on you. It's sort of like this jungle; it grows on everything. Make sure you take pictures everywhere you go. You may never have the opportunity again to go to the places that Ned's going to take you. You're a lucky girl."

"I will. And, yes, I am. I'm looking forward to this year; it's going to be great."

EIGHT
One Year Later

"What's the name of this place again, Ned?" MJ asked.

"Canillá. It's about fifty air miles northeast of Guatemala City. How's she looking now?"

"It looks like the flow is getting heavier," she answered. "I'll go back and check it from behind."

MJ walked to the cargo area and looked out the window at the number-two engine. A widening stream of black oil was flowing over the top

109

of the engine cowling, down over the wing, and departing the plane from the flap. MJ returned to her seat and strapped herself in.

"It's getting pretty thick, Ned, and we're smoking."

"What color is the smoke?" he asked her.

"White."

"Well, if it's got to smoke, I prefer white," he said. "I've reduced the power on both engines, a little more on the right side. So far, the temps and pressure are holding. I don't want to shut her down unless I have to."

"I can't believe this," MJ said. "I've been flying this bird for almost a year without any problems. And now, on my last trip, we're going to lose an engine."

"Last trip sounds a bit too final, MJ. Why don't we say it's your final sortie south of the border?" He looked at MJ and gave her a reassuring grin.

"Let's hope you're right. At least we're not flying over the jungles," she said. "Although I'm not sure this terrain is all that hospitable. It looks pretty rough."

"We'll be fine; we're heavy, but not that heavy. This Gooney flies pretty well on one. We've got a lot going for us: it's not super hot and humid, we're not overloaded, it will take a while before we lose all twenty-six gallons of oil from the tank, and Canillá is close to Guatemala City. We ought to be able to get some help with repairs in a couple of days—that might require a bit of luck, however."

"How come we never came here before?" she asked.

"Guatemala is very volatile. They are still messing with the Indians, trying to relocate them and move them off land the government wants to develop. It's risky bringing things in and out of this country; you never know who's in charge, or who might shoot at you on any given day. We're doing this run as a favor to one of our supporters. It seems that his daughter's school took on

111

this village as their missionary project for the year. They've been collecting money, food, and clothing for the better part of eight months. Her father called me and asked if I would haul it in here for them. I couldn't say 'No.' He's supported this work in Mexico and Central America for over fifteen years. That's a lot of pesos, MJ."

"I bet. Let's hope we don't disappoint him."

"There's San Cristóbal Veripaz, and there's Embalse Chixoy, the lake. Kind of hard to miss that lake, isn't it?" he said. "Canillá is just a little further west beyond the lake."

"That's a good thing," MJ said. "Oil pressure is beginning to drop and the engine temps are on the rise."

"OK. We don't want this to get any more expensive than necessary. Punch it out, MJ."

MJ pulled the throttle and prop levers back and brought the mixtures to idle cutoff. She reached up and pushed the feathering button on the overhead panel, then turned off the magnetos, the right generator, and the fuel selector. She checked the electrical load and vacuum; everything seemed to be functioning properly. The big prop windmilled for a couple of minutes and then came to a stop, the blades knifing through the oncoming air and looking quite statuesque.

Ned cranked in some left rudder and aileron trim to compensate for the loss of power on the right side. Although the Gooney Bird's remaining engine was still in cruise power, the plane began a slow, two-hundred-feet-per-minute descent.

"Any sign of fire?" Ned asked.

"No, none," she answered. "She's still smoking, but not as bad."

"The elevation hovers around three thousand in these parts. We'll bring her down to five thousand and give these wings a little more air to work with. I don't think we'll have any trouble holding our altitude at five," he said. "Get out the checklist just to make sure we didn't forget anything."

"Roger that."

She pulled out the checklist from between the seats and checked each item.

"Looks like we got everything," she said.

"Good. Just keep your eye on it to make sure we're not cooking. I don't want the natives to think some flaming chariot is descending on them, bringing hellfire and brimstone to their village."

"You've been hanging around these missionary types too long, Amigo," she said. "Maybe it's time you went Stateside for a little R&R."

"I don't think I would know what to do with the States or my time," he said. "I've grown accustomed to their customs. There's the village, just this side of the river. The landing strip is just a bit north of the village. How's that engine?"

"Just smoking, no fire," MJ reported.

"OK. Let's bring her in. There won't be a second chance on this one, MJ. We're too heavy to go around; you take it."

"Never a dull moment with you, is there?" she said. "From that first landing in a jungle cow pasture near Oaxaca, to landings on high plateaus. You're always putting me to the test. And now this: a single-engine approach, to an unfamiliar field, in the middle of nowhere."

"That's how you learn, Kiddo. That's how you learn. I got the before landing checks. Let me know what you want and when you want it."

MJ was surprised at how well the plane was handling with a dead engine and feathered prop. Even the load they were carrying didn't seem to make much of a difference to the Gooney. She was something, this workhorse. MJ set up for a crosswind at mid-field and called for gear down and the first notch of flaps.

It was quite a sight from the ground. As the sound of the P&W radial engine reached the village, people began emerging from their huts, tents, and buildings and looked skyward. What they saw was quite unexpected. The plane flew over the village toward the landing area, streaming a plume of white smoke in its wake. The scene was right out of World War II: a single plane returning from a mission over Europe with its engine shot out, hoping to make it to the safety of Dover before losing the other one. There was an immediate mass-migration from the village to the grass runway.

MJ turned onto the final approach course. "Flaps full, check gear, pressure, and boost pump," she ordered.

"Flaps are full, we've got the green, pressure's good," he said.

Ned reached over and pushed the gear lever down and watched the pressure on the gear system increase. The gear warning horn went off as he did this, jarring MJ's concentration. It ceased as soon as he returned the lever to neutral.

"I don't think I'll ever get used to that," she said.

"Put her in there, Captain," he said, ignoring her comment.

MJ trimmed the nose up slightly and further slowed the plane. Like many of the fields she had negotiated in the last year, this one was short and narrow. She wanted to slow the Gooney as much as possible without giving away her options and use as little of the strip as possible. She came in a little high and pulled the power on the one good engine, turning the plane into a glider and equalizing the forces affecting the approach. She took out the trim that Ned had put in on the rudder and aileron and wiggled the nose of the big bird with the rudders. The winds were calm, the air was cool, and the DC-3 floated over the threshold, its big balloon tires settling onto the sandy terrain.

"After stuff," she called out.

Ned took care of the after-landing routine and told MJ to carry a little extra speed on the rollout so they could spin the plane around without the help of the feathered engine. MJ let the plane roll almost to the end of the strip, brought it a little to the left, gunned the left engine and spun around to her right. She lined it up with the center of the rough landing strip and shut it down.

"Nice job," Ned offered.

"Thanks," she said. "Only one problem."

"What's that?" he asked.

"What do we do now?" she asked.

"Eat," he said.

"I mean about the engine. We can't get out of here on one."

"We'll deal with that later. First things first," he said. "I'm starving."

Ned unbuckled his seatbelt and walked to the back of the plane. He

118

opened one side of the cargo door and looked out at the small crowd of people that had gathered on the edge of the strip. A white-haired man in khaki clothes made his way to the front of the crowd and approached the plane.

"Are you OK?" he asked.

"We're fine, thanks," Ned assured him.

"That was quite a show," the man said.

"I bet it was," Ned replied.

"My name is Terry Shallock. I run the mission here. We've been expecting you ever since Mr. Halloway radioed that you would be delivering the things his daughter Melanie and her classmates had collected for us."

"Glad to do it," Ned said, climbing down the small ladder and extending a hand to Mr. Shallock. "I'm Ned Greenlawn. That's MJ," pointing to Mary Jane, as she appeared in the doorway. "She's the one that brought us in safe and sound."

"Nice to meet you both," Terry said. "We were just about to eat. Won't you join us?"

"I'd like nothing better," Ned said. "C'mon, MJ. You're in for a treat."

Ned, MJ, and Terry walked toward the waiting crowd. MJ felt as though she was about to walk into a rainbow, the native clothing was so colorful.

She remembered her first trip to Oaxaca, in the south of Mexico. It was the first time she had ever seen so much of the native dress, and it overwhelmed her. She used up a whole roll of film in that one village. Since that time, she had traveled to many villages in most of the Central American countries, where she experienced clothing, culture, and culinary art that was like nothing she had ever experienced before.

"After we eat, we'll get the people together and take the cargo off your plane," Terry said. "The children are very excited. It's like Christmas."

"I'd like to use your radio after we eat, too," Ned said. "I want to get a hold of a friend in Guatemala City and see what we can do for the old girl."

"You are most certainly welcome to use the radio," Terry offered. "It's the only connection we have to the outside. If it weren't for this airstrip, we'd be completely stranded during the rainy season; the road is impassable."

The group walked into the center of the village. The women returned to their various cooking fires. The aroma that filled the site was as sweet and delicious as any restaurant MJ had ever visited. Although Ned had warned her that it was going to be a difficult year, she found that the worst of her meals were from the vending machines in the FBOs at the major airports. Eating at the various remote villages was never a disappointment and always an adventure. In the past year, she had eaten things that she didn't know even existed; however, she was grateful that they waited until after the meal to fill her in on the details of the menu.

Terry led them over to a table set beneath a thatched roof—a pavilion, of sorts. Some of the women began bringing an assortment of plates from the various cooking fires and placed them on the table. MJ watched a buffet fit for royalty appear in front of her. They seemed to lack nothing in the way of culinary delights.

"Enjoy," Terry said. "They have prepared some special dishes for you. They don't get too many visitors, especially ones that bring them a planeload of gifts. They are very hospitable people."

"I can see that," Ned said. "I'm not sure I'll be able to do too much if I eat all this food. I'll be ready for a siesta."

"Well, you're in luck," Terry said. "That's exactly the next thing on the agenda."

"I'd better try to call someone first," Ned said. "But, after that, I could use a good snooze."

After the meal, Ned went with Terry to use the radio in Terry's headquarters. He was gone for over an hour. MJ used her time to help clean up and take a group of people to the plane to begin unloading the supplies. Ned arrived halfway through the project.

"We're in luck, MJ," Ned reported. "I got a hold of a guy from the US who's at the army base just outside Guatemala City. He picks up and delivers DC-3s all over the region, and he's a mechanic, to boot. One of my contacts happened to be working with him today, so I was able to talk directly to the mechanic about our problem. The officer he works with on the base has agreed to lend him a truck and some supplies. He said it will take a couple of days, but he'll be here."

"That's great!" MJ exclaimed. "Although I don't think I would mind hanging out here for a week or so. These people are great, and that meal was something else. Maybe I'll

go into the restaurant business
instead of freight hauling when I
get back to the US from this
adventure. I've got enough new
recipes to last me a lifetime."

"That's fine for you, but I've got
a lot of flying left to do this
month. We've got to get back to
Mexico City by the end of the week,
if we can; I've got a new copilot to
break-in."

"You found someone?"

"Sort of."

"Another woman?"

"Fat chance. There will never be
another one like you, MJ. A guy
doesn't get this lucky more than
once in his life. No, it's some guy
out of Atlanta who wants to build
his multiengine time. Another one of
our more benevolent benefactors has
called in a chit. I told him I'd
give the guy a shot, but I'm not too
enthusiastic about it. He's very
young, low time, and hasn't had the
most successful flying career of his
young life. Seems he banged up a
Cessna 150 on his first solo, had a

gear-up landing in an Arrow, and mushed an Aztec in after losing an engine on take-off. The only reason I agreed to take him on is that his dad is a friend of our benefactor and has offered a substantial amount of money to our operation if I take him on for a year. This could turn out to be the longest year of my career—if I live through it."

"Ned, if anyone can teach this guy something, it's you," MJ said. "On the other hand, I bet you won't be taking as many futon snoozes as I've allowed you."

"Speaking of snoozes, let's get the rest of this stuff off the plane and grab a siesta. We haven't had much sleep lately, and I could use a bunch."

"Works for me," MJ said. "We've gotten to the middle of the load; it shouldn't take much longer."

NINE

"Otto A. Sanderson, at your service," the driver said, as he climbed out of the old, Guatemalan Army deuce-and-a-half. "Like my wheels?"

"I love your wheels and *you*," Ned said, grabbing his hand and shaking it warmly. "I can't believe we were lucky enough to have someone like you so close."

"So close?" Otto asked. "You obviously haven't traveled these roads, especially in one of these tanks."

"No, I can't say that I have, or that I want to, either," Ned answered.

"It's a good thing that it's the dry season, too," Otto said. "There would be no way in hell to get over those roads in the rainy season. I suppose we could have flown something in here, but that's not always possible, either. It gets pretty nasty here: heavy rain, low clouds, mountain obscuration. It's a bush pilot's nightmare."

"I'm sure it is," Ned responded. "Do you want something to eat or drink?"

"I could use some water, but I ate some stuff on the way. Where's the bird?"

"She's parked on the strip, over there," he said and pointed in the direction of the plane. "I'll grab some water and meet you there."

"Great!"

Otto jumped back into the truck and drove over to the plane. He shut down the engine, walked around to the back, and lowered the backstop. He leaned up against the back of the truck and looked back toward the village for Ned.

"Hi there!" MJ said, as she walked up behind Otto.

"Key-riced," Otto said, as he spun around and fell over his feet. "You scared the shit out of me. You shouldn't be sneaking up on people like that, especially out here in the middle of nowhere."

"Sorry," MJ apologized. "You always this nervous?"

"South of the border?" he asked. "Damn straight. There are too many built-in surprises down here for someone to get too comfortable."

"I'm Mary Jane Carlson," MJ said. She offered her hand to Otto.

"Otto Sanderson. You a pilot?"

"Uh-huh," MJ responded, half expecting some smart-ass remark to follow.

"Yeah, me too," Otto said enthusiastically. "Don't you just love these things?"

"I'm beginning to, especially now that I've seen how well they do on one engine," MJ answered.

"They just don't want to quit flying, it seems," Otto said.

"That's a good thing," MJ said.

"Which one did you lose?" Otto asked.

"The right one. It was throwing a lot of oil and smoking pretty badly."

"OK. I'll take a look at it."

"So, you're a mechanic, too?"

"Yup. I never know when I'm going to get a flying job, so I make sure I have something else to help me keep groceries in the cupboard."

Otto walked back to the truck and got in, started it, and drove it around to the other side of the plane. Under MJ's watchful eye, he backed the deuce-and-a-half up to the right engine so that he could use the back end to stand on for his inspection. He climbed onto the back of the truck and retrieved his tools from up by the headboard. After removing the engine cowling, he began inspecting each of the cylinders, searching for the source of the problem.

"This looks like the culprit," he said.

He returned to his tool kit and pulled out a few more wrenches. After about an hour-and-a-half, he had an engine cylinder lying on the back of the truck and open for their inspection.

"It's got a pretty good crack in it," Otto said. "Fortunately, it doesn't look like there's any damage to any other components. From what you told me over the radio, I was hoping that this was all that it was. Looks like I guessed right."

"Can you fix it?" MJ asked.

"Fix it? No," he said. "Replace it? Now, that's another thing." He winked at Ned and gave MJ a grin.

Otto jumped into the back of the truck and went up toward the headboard to a large tarp covering a pile of something. He pulled the tarp and revealed a complete Pratt and Whitney 1830P engine strapped to a pallet.

"Of course I had to come prepared for any contingency. I don't often guess right," he said. I'll just pull one of the jugs off this thing and replace the one you blew. You should be on your way by sometime tomorrow. How about oil? Do you need any?"

"Oil is something we have plenty of," Ned answered. "This beauty leaks so much of it, we wouldn't leave home without fifty gallons or so."

"Smart thinking," Otto said. "I could use one of you to help with some of this, if you can spare the time."

"I'll do it," MJ offered. "If I'm going to go into business for myself and depend on a Doug to pay my bills, I had better learn as much as I can about her."

"Great. It'll just make it go a little faster with a go-for helping," Otto said.

"Gopher?" MJ asked.

"You know, go-for-this, go-for-that," he said.

"I see," she said. "Well, I won't mind the temporary title of 'Go-for', as long as you explain what you're doing when I'm not 'go-for-ing.'"

"Deal," Otto said.

Ned returned to the village to radio Antonio in Tepotzlan and let him know that they would be back in a day or two. MJ sat on the wing, resting her back against the fuselage, watching Otto put the engine back together and asking questions.

"Did I hear you say that you are going to go into business for yourself?" Otto asked.

"Yeah. I'm not interested in the major airlines . . . too stuffy. I'd like to continue doing what I've been doing. I like it," she said.

"That's going to cost some bucks," he said.

"Yup. I've got some money that I invested before coming down here, and it's done well since I've been gone. My folks said that they would help me with a loan if I needed it. I made a lot of contacts while flying freight out of Billings, too."

"Montana," Otto interrupted. "Billings, Montana?"

"Yes. Billings, Montana. I grew up not too far from there and spent a few years flying out of a Billings airport."

"I've always wanted to go to Montana," he said. "All the pictures I've seen look like dreamscapes."

"That's probably because most travel brochures use pictures of the mountains, especially Glacier National Park. The eastern half of the state is rather boring," she said.

"I still want to go there someday. Ever since I was a kid, I've wanted to go there and be a cowboy. Hand me that jug, will you please?"

"Well, hang in. Maybe you'll make it up there. If you do, I can give you some names of folks you could stay with—pilot friends," she said, as she picked up the top of the cylinder jug and handed it to him.

"You got a partner?" Otto asked.

"Hadn't thought about that," she answered. "Why? You interested?"

"I'm getting tired of these trips down here, to tell you the truth. I wouldn't be disappointed if I gave up this act. I've had it up to here with the red tape, bureaucratic bullshit, and palm greasing that has to go on all of the time. You can't get anything done without paying somebody something, and that only gets you a piece of paper to get you out of your current situation. As soon as you arrive at your next stop, you find out they want *another* piece of paper, and that's going to cost you, too. It's a bit much, if you ask me."

"So you're looking for other work?" she asked.

"You might say that."

"You have your A&P?" she asked.

"Yup. I'm official. Even down here you need the documentation to get things signed-off properly. The International Civil Aviation Organization, or ICAO, keeps a tight reign on things, in spite of governmental shenanigans. You *might* be able to buy a signature from the aviation authorities down here, but it's not likely. Not like paying the 'mordida'—the bite, or bribe—in Mexico. So, yeah, I'm a pedigree, with the papers to prove it."

"It *would* be nice to have a partner with a pedigree. It might save the company a few dollars in maintenance costs, too," she said.

135

"Why don't you give me a number where I can reach you in the States? When I get things better organized, I'll give you a call to see if you're still interested."

"Fair enough. Were you able to get your type rating for the Gooney while you were down here?"

"Yes, as a matter of fact," she answered. "We had a lull about six months ago, so Ned prepared me and set up a check ride with a Mexican examiner."

"How's that going to work in the States?" he asked.

"From what I understand, I just need to take the Mexican paperwork to the local Flight Standards District Office, and they'll take care of it. At least, I hope that's all. Who knows? Dealing with the FAA isn't exactly a walk-in-the-park, either. We'll see. I have a few other things to worry about, first."

"I hope you do it. It would be nice to get in on the ground floor of a charter outfit," he said. "OK, that should do it. You said you have oil?"

"Sure. Let me get it."

MJ climbed down off the wing and went to the back of the plane. She grabbed a container of oil and brought it around to Otto, who was up on the wing opening the oil filler cap. She climbed onto the back of the truck and handed it up to him, then headed for the cockpit. She sat herself in the right seat and stuck her head out of the window, watching as Otto finished pouring the oil into the well.

"I'm ready when you are," she said.

"Just a minute. I want to get around front where I can see the cylinders."

Otto climbed down off the wing, moved the truck forward away from the plane, and placed himself where he could see the engine and MJ could see him.

"OK," he said. "Don't give it any primer or boost or spark. I just want you to turn the blades with the starter until we're sure we have some oil circulating."

MJ rotated the props until Otto held up his hand for her to stop.

"OK, MJ. Fire it up."

MJ went through the start procedure and the engine came to life, emitting a billowing cloud of smoke.

"Don't worry," he yelled, over the noise of the engine. "That's just the excess oil that was in the cylinder we were working on."

MJ set the throttle to idle and looked back at the number two engine. The smoke diminished after a few minutes, and the engine was idling smoothly. Otto signaled her to increase the power. She made sure that the parking brake was set and moved the throttle forward to 1700 · rpms. Otto watched the spinning blades and called for more power. MJ moved the lever forward until she had 2000 rpms. Otto stood with his arms folded over his chest and casually watched the engine roar its approval of the new cylinder. Otto ran his hand across his throat, indicating it was time for her to reduce the power. She brought the power back to idle and looked at him again. He motioned her to cut the engine.

"Sounds good to me," he said, after the props had come to a halt. How are the gauges behaving?"

"Pressure and temperature were fine. She sounds like new."

"She *is* new," he said, grinning. "At least part of her is."

MJ climbed out of the cockpit and walked down the fuselage to the cargo door. She climbed down the ladder and walked around the front of the plane and over to the truck. Otto was putting his tools back in place.

"Thanks," she said.

"You're welcome. I'm going to get cleaned up, then I'll get you a couple of numbers where you can reach me in the States. I think this could be interesting," he said.

"Will you be going right back to Guatemala City?" she asked.

"No. It's too late. These roads are treacherous in the daytime. At night you have to watch out for the holes, the cows, and the bandits," he answered.

"*Bandits*?" she asked.

"Bandidos," he said. "It's like the Wild West around here. These people have little or nothing, and here I am driving around in a government truck, the symbol of tyranny. No, I think I'll wait until morning. It's too easy to get ambushed at night."

"I guess I missed all that by flying from place to place," MJ said.

"Be thankful that you did. It can get pretty hairy at times. That's another reason I'd like to return and stay up north. I'm no hero."

Ned walked up from the direction of the village and met the two of them walking back.

"All set?" he asked them both.

"All set," they answered, almost in unison.

"Will she get us back to Mexico?" Ned asked Otto.

"She will unless she gets another sick cylinder," Otto assured him. "How many hours on these engines?"

"Don't ask," Ned said. "We take as good care of her as we can, Otto. Limited funds and all that, you know."

"Yeah, I know. Just don't let it limit your life," Otto said. "Get me your engine log, and I'll sign off the work. I'll also need an address where we can send a bill. I'd like to offer my services gratis for you, but it's not my company, nor my say. Maybe they'll cut you some slack if you tell them what you do down here. It doesn't hurt to ask."

"I understand," Ned said. "And, no, it doesn't hurt to ask. Most people have been very generous with us. We'll take what we can get.

141

Thanks for helping us out; I'm sure you did a great job."

"You're welcome," Otto said. "Have a safe flight. Maybe we'll see each other again someday."

"You never know," Ned answered. "You just never know."

PART TWO

Rick Byam

TEN

Mary Jane Carlson tucked her dirty-blonde hair into her baseball cap and pulled the ponytail through the opening in the back. She donned her work gloves over her tan hands and grabbed the fuel dipstick before climbing the ladder onto the right wing of the olive drab DC-3. She climbed to inspect the twenty-six gallon oil reservoir that fed the engine to keep it cool and functioning; oil slicks from the leaking Pratt & Whitney 1830P rotary engines made it slippery going. Satisfied that the quantity of oil would see them through the next leg

of their trip, she replaced the
filler cap and secured it. She
turned and opened the filler cap for
the main fuel tank and checked the
quantity with the fuel stick. It
showed one hundred gallons
remaining. Securing the cap, she
moved toward the back of the wing
and removed the cap for the
auxiliary tank and checked it. It
was full at two hundred gallons. She
calculated five hours and fifteen
minutes of flying with a forty-five
minute reserve, assuming about fifty
gallons per hour of fuel burn. That
also assumed that the auto-lean
carburetor function was working
properly, something that didn't
always happen.

"Don't believe the gauges," she
reminded herself. "Always dip the
tanks at each stop."

She climbed down the ladder and
dragged it behind her, creeping
under the dirty belly of the old
Gooney Bird to set up for the same
tasks on the left wing. Checking the
oil level on the left engine, she
found it was below the opening of
the baffles used to determine the
quantity of oil in each tank. She

climbed down the ladder to get a spare can of the murky, 50-weight lubricant they carried with them in the back of the plane.

"Yo, MJ! You want something to eat?" yelled Otto, her copilot, from the door of the FBO—the fixed base operator where goods and services were provided for pilots.

"Yeah, sure. Grab me one of those ugly ham and cheese sandwiches that's been sitting in the vending machine for the last week and a Diet Coke. That ought to get me to Phoenix."

"That might get you to Phoenix, MJ, but I'll bet you'll spend most of the trip in the back trying to keep your butt over the waste basket at ten-thousand feet!" Otto screamed back over the whine of a Falcon jet that had just begun its startup. "I'm going to take the courtesy car and buzz up the road to Subway. I don't want my captain out of the cockpit when things start getting busy on the approach end of this run. I'll be back before the freight arrives."

147

"Fine!" Mary Jane yelled fruitlessly, giving him thumbs up to show she got the message. She knew he couldn't hear her over the whining, CF700 jet engines of the Falcon.

MJ returned to her preflight duties. She filled the oil reservoir on the number one engine to capacity and took note that she was burning a good bit of crude on this side. She would have to note it on the maintenance squawk sheet before finishing the trip. After climbing down and securing the ladder in the tail end of the aircraft, she walked under the belly of the beast and began to sump the fuel tanks. It was cold last night, so she was sure there would be a bit of water in the fuel from condensation. She was right, and it took a couple of minutes for her to drain the water that had collected in the bottom of each tank. She was surprised at just how cold the night was; after all, they were in El Paso, Texas, as close as you can get to the Mexican border. It had been an unusual spring so far, but it seemed unnatural to be freezing on the border this late in April.

"Oh well," she mused. "We'll be baking in Phoenix before you know it."

She walked around the rest of the airplane, checking to make sure that everything was in place and all was secure. She checked the tires and brakes and then looked up into the wheel-well for leaks or unusual quantities of oil. These old sky trains were known for leaking oil from every possible orifice, and then some. Nonetheless, MJ had learned over her fifteen years of driving these birds just how much was too much. "If the puddle of oil under the engine is small enough to jump across, it's still safe to fly," she thought, remembering a humorous adage she heard many times about the leaky P&W engines. Satisfied, she removed her gloves, climbed into the aircraft, and worked her way to the cockpit. The freight wasn't due for another hour, so she plunked herself down into one of the jump seats, put her feet up on the divider, and closed her eyes.

It was about an hour later when Otto quietly ascended the bird's ladder and tiptoed up the slanted floor to the cockpit. Taking careful aim, he dropped MJ's lunch into her lap from as high as he could. The results were instantaneous. MJ swung her elbows out to both sides but found no target. Otto knew the routine and moved himself from harm's way.

"What the . . . " she mumbled as she dropped her legs to the floor, letting her bagged lunch drop to the deck. "What the hell's wrong with you? Moron!" she spit vehemently at Otto. "I could've broken my elbow, you Dork."

"Nah," he mumbled back, as he stuffed another bite of a roast beef and cheese hoagie into his already full mouth. "I've done it to you a hundred times, and you never hit anything. At least you haven't after the first time, when you got me square in the cojones. I learned quickly after that."

"You had better knock that shit off real soon, Buster, or you might just find yourself taking some air without a chute on one of these legs." She retrieved her sandwich and Coke from the floor. "Has the freight arrived yet?"

"I don't think so. I didn't see any trucks hanging around that weren't hanging around before," he said between gulps of his Dr. Pepper. "Who are we hauling for, anyway?"

"It's a new account," she said, unwrapping the sandwich and inspecting the contents. "Didn't you get any mustard for this thing?"

"You didn't ask for any," he said, shrugging his shoulders.

"Otto, how long have we been flying together?" she asked.

"Too many years to remember, Boss."

"And how many times do you think I've eaten these ham and cheese delights over that time?"

"Sorry, Cap, that's not something I keep in my logbook."

"Take a shot at it, Otto. How many of these things do you think I've devoured?"

"Over all those years?" he said. "Well, I guess you must have had at least a few million."

"All right. So how many of those came with mustard?" she said as she glared into his round face with its tiny nose and hazel eyes.

"How the hell am I supposed to know, MJ?" he shot back, tired of this conversation.

"All of them," she said. "*All* of them, Otto. So why, now, do you decide that I don't need mustard?"

This was getting to be too much for Otto. He knew that she was tired and hadn't slept much in the last week. But to get so bent out of shape over mustard, on a sandwich that wouldn't taste much like a sandwich after sitting in a bag for a couple of hours, was a clear indication that it was time to vacate the premises.

"MJ, get your own lunch next time. I'm going back and check on the freight," he said over his shoulder, heading for the door.

MJ looked at the sandwich, put it back together, wrapped it up, put it back into the bag, and tossed it onto the seat where she had been napping.

"*Too* much," she grumbled.

ELEVEN

MJ stowed her sandwich in the cooler and climbed out of the big DC-3 into the hot El Paso sun. The tarmac was already simmering and throwing heat waves that distorted the view of the FBO just fifty yards away. She walked in that direction and went through her mental checklist, making sure that she hadn't forgotten anything. She opened the door and felt the cool air sweep across her face, wondering how anyone ever lived in this place before air-conditioning. "It must have been unbearable," she thought. The smell of coffee and fresh popcorn filled her senses. She resisted the urge for more coffee with all the self-control she could muster; she already had two cups this morning and more caffeine would mean an uncomfortable ride to Phoenix. She settled for drinking in the aroma of the fresh roast.

"Any word on our freight?" she yelled across the room to Jack, the owner and operator of the flight services on the field.

"Yeah, MJ," he yelled back. "They just called. Said they were just leaving and should be here in about thirty minutes."

"Thanks. Let's hope they are, or I'm going to have trouble getting out of here. It's getting pretty steamy."

MJ picked up the phone and dialed Flight Service. Experience had taught her that immediately punching the number 1 on the touch-tone pad would pre-empt the usual preliminary messages. A preflight briefer answered at once.

"Albuquerque Flight Service, good morning," chimed the cheerful voice on the other end of the line.

"Good morning," she passed back. "I'd like to file a flight plan."

"Sure thing. Go ahead."

MJ began the familiar chant, "IFR. She is November one eight Mike Juliet, a DC-3 slash Uniform, 140 knots, with a little help from our friends. We're out of Echo Lima Papa this morning at 15Z, 10,000 feet to El Paso VOR, then Victor 94 to Totec, then Victor one-six, direct Phoenix, Papa, X-Ray, Romeo. It should be two hours and thirty minutes. We have a VFR GPS on board and six hours and zero minutes of fuel. No alternate today, Mary Jane Carlson, on file at Bravo India Lima, 800-555-6329, two souls on board. This buzzard is olive drab from nose to tail."

"OK," the briefer said, after a bit of a pause as she typed in the remaining information. "Would you like a weather briefing?"

"No, thanks. I checked the DTN and it looks like severe clear the whole way. How about checking Notams D for me, though?"

"Standby one."

After a pause, the briefer came back and reported that there were no Notices to Airmen for her route of flight.

"Is there anything else I can do for you this morning?" the briefer said, continuing with her cheerful demeanor.

"No. I guess not," said MJ. "Thanks."

"Have a good flight," she said.

MJ looked out the window toward her plane and saw a large yellow truck backing up to the cargo door under the direction of Otto's watchful eye. She pulled out her cell phone and a piece of paper from the right pocket of her coveralls.

"Good morning," she said to the party on the other end. "This is Mary Jane Carlson. The freight has

157

just arrived, and we should be airborne in about twenty minutes. It's about two-and-a-half hours en route; so we should be arriving just about on time."

She listened for a couple of minutes and then disconnected, placing the cell phone and paper back into her coveralls. She made one last pit stop in the ladies room before walking out into the grueling West Texas sun.

"I'll be glad when we reach cruising altitude and cooler temps," she thought, as she walked toward the plane. "This is just too damn hot too early in the morning for me."

"Morning, Ma'am," the man standing at the back of the truck said as MJ approached.

"Morning," she smiled back. "You have some paperwork for me?"

"Sure thing, Ma'am. I've got it right here."

MJ looked over the papers, signed one of them, and handed them back to the driver.

The driver looked over the paperwork and then looked up at MJ with a big grin on his face.

"Do you know that your name in Spanish is Marijuana?" he laughed. "Maybe that's what you should be hauling around in your ugly airplane; then you could afford to buy a new, faster one and have more work and more money in your pockets."

"You think so?" she fired back at him. "Maybe I should take a look and see what's in these crates. What do you think, Amigo?"

"Suit yourself. I just haul whatever they put on my truck. If somebody finds something wrong with the load, I just give him the papers and the keys. As far as I'm concerned, if I have papers, I'm not responsible for the cargo. It's the guys who fill out the paperwork that will pay the price. Me, I'm just the burro, if you know what I mean."

MJ did know what he meant; however, as pilot-in-command and president of her own company, it was her butt that was going to fry if anything was out of order.

"It must be nice not to have to worry," she said to him, as he made his way back to the cab.

"Oh, I worry plenty," he said over his shoulder. "I just don't worry about this job, driving things from here to there. I worry about bigger things, things that make a world of difference."

MJ looked after him for a minute longer, trying to discern his meaning. However, she didn't have the luxury of discussing philosophy with him just now; she had a shipment to deliver.

"Hey, Otto!" she yelled into the back of the plane. "Make sure you get these skids as close to the front as you can. We've got to have room for another three waiting for us in Phoenix."

"No problem, Cap!" Otto yelled back, over the whining of the electric winch he was using to pull the last of the three skids up the steel plated incline of the old tail-dragger. "As long as the weight works out, we're golden."

"Hey, MJ," Otto said, as he was strapping the last pallet to the deck. "Did that guy seem a little strange to you?"

"In what way?" she asked.

"Oh, I don't know. I thought he was Mexican. You know, with the nice tan face, mustache, and all. But the more he talked to me, the more I began to think that he wasn't. He had a strange accent. Actually, I don't think it was his accent; it was more like a different intonation in his voice."

"What difference does it make, Otto? This is El Paso; there are all kinds of folks who work here and across the border," she said matter-of-factly.

"Didn't you say this was a new account? We haven't hauled for these people before, have we?" Otto quizzed, with a slight hint of concern in his voice.

"Nope," came her quick reply. "But they paid cash up front and they weren't asking us to haul any hazardous materials. That's two points in their favor, as far as I'm concerned."

"What's the total on the weight?" Otto asked, jumping down from the fuselage.

"Just a bit over four thousand pounds," she answered. "We'd better get airborne before it gets any hotter, or we're going to have to wait until after dark; that would really screw things up. Let's go!"

MJ climbed the short ladder into the plane and made her way to the left seat of the cockpit. Otto hustled around outside the plane pulling the chocks and control locks from the elevator, rudder, and ailerons. MJ flipped the master battery switch, threw the avionics power switch to "On," and dialed up clearance delivery on the #1 radio. She slipped her David Clark headset on over her baseball cap, tuned in the Automated Terminal Information Service on COM2 and copied down the information. She then switched the radio back to COM1 and clearance delivery, listened for a break in the conversation, and squeezed her push-to-talk switch.

"El Paso clearance," she said into her microphone, "November one eight Mike Juliet, IFR to Phoenix with delta."

"November one eight Mike Juliet," the controller responded, "cleared as filed to the Phoenix International Airport. Climb and maintain eight thousand feet, expect ten thousand ten minutes after departure, departure frequency will be one two four point two five, squawk six three four five."

"November one eight Mike Juliet understands cleared as filed to Papa Hotel X-Ray, eight thousand, ten in ten, twenty-four twenty-five, six three four five," MJ read back to the controller.

"Read-back correct," the controller responded. "Contact ground, point-niner."

MJ switched the avionics power switch and the master battery switch off and removed her headset. Otto was just pulling in the ladder and closing the cargo doors.

"Ottoman!" MJ yelled back to him. "Double check those tie-downs and make sure that nothing is wiggling. We don't need any of this stuff sliding to our tail."

"Done!" Otto yelled back, as he tugged at each of the tie-downs holding the freight in place.

Otto closed the cockpit door behind him and took his place in the right seat.

"Are we all set, Boss?" he asked, strapping himself in and grabbing his headset.

"Yup. Got our clearance. We just need to crank her up and head on out. Give me the list."

Otto began reading from the checklist, calling out each item as MJ acknowledged the item and its condition. When the checklist was complete, MJ switched on the beacon light.

"Give me nine blades on that right engine and make sure the cowl flaps are open and off," she said to Otto, while throwing the switches for the electric fuel boost pumps. She reached up and hit the starter and primer at the same time.

"Six," Otto called.

MJ reached up with her other hand and turned on the magnetos for the right engine, as Otto called the 9th propeller, indicating that the engine was free of hydraulic lock. The engine fired, then hesitated, fired again, and roared to life. MJ reached over and moved the mixture control from idle cutoff to auto-rich and released the starter switch. She kept her finger on the primer just in case the big engine decided it didn't have enough fuel to keep running. She moved her hand to the throttle and set the rpms to one thousand, checked the oil pressure and temperatures, and then turned her attention to the left engine. She repeated the process until both engines were humming the same tune and she was satisfied that the big Pratt and Whitney 1830 rotary engines were functioning as they should.

"Who's driving?" Otto chimed in, as they checked their headsets and intercom system.

"I'll take this leg," she said, as her hands continued to move over the controls, fine tuning aileron and rudder trim and engine settings. "You be the copilot person; I'll do it out of Phoenix."

"Ten-four, Good Buddy," he grinned back at her, as he reached for the push-to-talk switch on the column in front of him.

"I'm not your 'good buddy,' Ottoman. Do that talkin' thing you do and get us out of here."

"El Paso Ground, November one eight Mike Juliet, Precision Air, ready to taxi," Otto rattled off into his mic.

"November one eight Mike Juliet, El Paso ground. Taxi to runway two-two by way of Uniform, Lima, Mike,

Kilo, Juliet. Hold short two-six left; acknowledge hold short instructions," the controller said quickly and clearly.

"Taxi two-two; Uniform, Lima, Mike, Kilo, Juliet; hold short two-six left; November one eight Mike Juliet," Otto repeated just as quickly and clearly.

"Check our right side," MJ instructed, as she released the parking brake and tail wheel and began moving the throttles forward.

"Clear, Cap," Otto responded.

MJ's feet began to paddle back and forth on the big rudder pedals. She jockeyed the big bird out onto the taxiway and toward the departing runway; the DC-3 squeaked and creaked its way along. MJ juggled the throttles to help keep the plane on the centerline. This was the hardest part of flying these things . . . taxiing, especially when there was a strong crosswind. The large rudder was an expert at grabbing all the wind it could and making your life miserable, especially in a crosswind. It was the P&W engines that kept you honest on those days.

"Cleared to cross two-six left," the controller radioed to them before they reached the hold short point.

"Cleared over two-six left, one eight Mike Juliet," Otto acknowledged.

MJ stopped the big bird just short of the hold line for runway two-two and applied the parking brake. In colder climates, they would have had to wait for the oil and cylinder head temps to hit forty-eight and one hundred degrees centigrade respectively before taxiing. However, the South Texas sun had warmed the oil, and they were able to proceed without delay. MJ checked the vacuum and pushed the throttles forward until she had 1700 rpms. She began cycling the props, moving the prop handles back until the rpms dropped about two hundred, and then pushed them full forward to the stops. She moved the handles aft again, until the rpms dropped about four hundred, then pushed the levers full forward. On the final swing, she brought the levers all the way back and waited until the rpms bottomed out and stabilized, somewhere around 1200 rpms, before pushing them forward to the stops. Next, she pushed the feathering switch for the right engine and watched the voltmeter for movement, indicating the generator was picking up a load. Noting it was working properly, she pulled the switch out and repeated the procedure for the left engine. Both were feathering properly. The final step was to bring the prop handles back to the stops one final time to make sure that the governor was still working as it should.

ATIS was reporting the altimeter setting at 30.12, so MJ ran the throttles individually to thirty inches of manifold pressure to check the magnetos. Otto watched the right engine for vibration as MJ threw the mag switch, first to the left mag, back to "both", then the right one, and back to "both." MJ checked the drop on the tachometer. She repeated the exercise for the left engine, although it was her turn to watch for engine vibration while Otto checked for rpm drop. MJ brought the throttles back to idle. She re-checked the engine gauges; everything looked to be within normal limits.

"You all set, Otto?" she asked as she released the parking brake.

"You bet. Same old, same old."

"Roger that. If anything happens before V1, we abort. After that, we treat it as an in-flight emergency. I fly, you cry. I'll handle the throttles and prop; you get the gear and the after takeoff stuff. Any questions? Anything I've left out?"

This routine was followed flight after flight; it was necessary to make sure that they both knew their responsibilities, especially if there was a problem. It was the last check before launching—the last chance to make sure they survived the departure.

"You got it all, MJ," Otto said as he adjusted his seat and seatbelt. "Good morning El Paso Tower! Gooney Bird November one eight Mike Juliet, number one for departure runway two-two."

"Douglas one eight Mike Juliet, cleared for takeoff runway two-two. Fly runway heading."

"Runway heading, cleared to go, Mike Juliet," Otto repeated.

Otto switched the transponder from standby to altitude reporting, flipped the strobe lights on, moved the actuators that controlled the cowl flaps from open to trail, and turned on the electric fuel boost pumps. MJ maneuvered the ship onto the centerline of runway two-two, locked the tail wheel in place, and advanced the throttles. Otto tapped her hand as she approached the target power setting and adjusted the throttles to the manifold pressure she had chosen for takeoff.

"Gear up," she called, as the plane climbed beyond any useful runway remaining.

At five hundred feet above the ground, MJ pulled the throttles back to METO, the maximum except takeoff power setting, and pulled the prop levers back until the rpms read 2550.

Otto reached for the gear-locking lever near the right side of MJ's seat on the floor. He released the locking ring, pulled the lever straight up, then grabbed the gear lever next to him, pulling it out and up to the retract position. At one thousand feet, MJ adjusted the power to thirty-six inches of manifold pressure and the props to 2325 rpm, calling for the after stuff. Otto switched one boost pump off and then the other. He watched the fuel pressure gauges stabilize under the direction of the engine fuel pumps. He checked the gear down pressure and noted it read zero. He looked out his window to make sure the gear fully retracted, and then put the gear handle back to the neutral position.

"November one eight Mike Juliet, contact departure, one twenty-four twenty-five," the tower controller directed the flight.

"Over to departure," Otto shot back.

Otto switched frequencies, listened, and then keyed his mic.

"Departure, November one eight Mike Juliet climbing through five point five for eight."

"November one eight Mike Juliet, El Paso departure. Radar contact. Climb to eight thousand feet, fly heading three five zero to intercept victor ninety-four," the new controller responded.

"Three five zero to intercept, eight thousand," Otto repeated.

MJ trimmed the plane for a 110 knot climb, while Otto talked to departure and finished the after takeoff checklist. She sat back, crossed her arms, and looked over at Otto.

"Well, Ottoman, here we go again."

"You know, MJ, I don't think I'll ever get tired of this scene. This big, old, beautiful bird will probably carry me to my grave," Otto said as he got COM2 ready for the anticipated call to Center.

"Let's hope that means this bird will be carrying your casket and won't *become* your casket," she responded.

"Mike Juliet, contact Albuquerque Center on one two eight point two. Good day," said the controller.

"One two eight point two. See ya," Otto called back and switched over to the #2 radio.

"Albuquerque Center, November one eight Mike Juliet, eight thousand," Otto reported to the new controller.

"November one eight Mike Juliet, roger," came the reply. "Climb and maintain ten thousand, one zero thousand."

"Out of eight for ten, Mike Juliet," Otto repeated.

MJ began leveling the big machine at nine thousand five hundred and had it trimmed for cruise by the time they reached ten thousand feet. She let the airspeed build to 140 knots, then brought the manifold pressure back to twenty-eight inches and pulled the prop levers to the cruise setting of 2050 rpm. She waited the obligatory five minutes for the engine temperatures to stabilize and then moved the mixture levers to auto-lean. The Gooney Bird was doing what it did best . . . lumber along with a belly half-full of freight and two contented pilots who asked for nothing more in life than to fly her.

TWELVE

"Douglas, November one eight Mike Juliet, contact Albuquerque Center on one three four point four five."

The controller's voice leaped inside of MJ's daydream and yanked her back to reality.

"Um, thirty-four twenty-five," MJ responded to the instructions.

"That's one three four point forty-five, four five," corrected the controller. "Have a nice day."

"Point four five. Thanks, you too. See ya," croaked MJ, as she tuned the standby frequency to the newly assigned one, pushed it over to "use" from "standby" and keyed her mic. "Albuquerque, Gooney bird November one eight Mike Juliet checking in. Ten thousand."

"One eight Mike Juliet, Albuquerque, roger. Altimeter three zero point one two," replied the new controller.

"Three zero one two," repeated MJ.

"Hey, Sleeping Beauty!" MJ yelled over her shoulder to a napping Otto who was laid out on a Futon they kept in the plane for such purposes. "Rise and shine, Flyboy!"

Otto rolled over on his side and propped himself up on one elbow, rubbing the sleep out of his eyes with his other hand. "Are we there yet, Captain?"

"Coming up on Totec intersection; they're going to turn us inbound soon. Give the freight a look-see. Make sure everything is tied down nice and cozy-like. Then get your

177

butt up here. I wouldn't want the
FAA to find my copilot fast asleep
when we pull up to the ramp and they
yank open the door.

"Never happen, Cap," Otto yawned
back to MJ. "It's broad daylight.
Those vampires never come out until
the sun goes down. Matter of fact, I
don't think they roll out until at
least two o'clock in the morning."

"Always expect the unexpected,
Ottoman!" MJ shouted over her
shoulder. "It would be just our luck
to get nailed with a ramp check in
the middle of the day when we least
expect it. I still have bills to
pay; I can't afford to keep this
bird on the ground any longer than
necessary, let alone pay the Feds a
fine or two!"

"November one eight Mike Juliet,
Albuquerque. Descend and maintain
five thousand five hundred until
Totec, then five thousand. Contact
Phoenix Approach on one two six
point eight. So long."

"Down to fifty-five hundred to
cross Totec, then five thousand.

Phoenix on one two six point eight. Talk to you later."

MJ repeated the instructions to the Albuquerque controller while dialing up the new frequency on standby. After bidding farewell to the Albuquerque controller, she pushed the flip-flop switch on the COM1 panel that put the Phoenix controller's frequency in the active mode.

"Phoenix Approach, November one eight Mike Juliet descending through seven point five for five point five," MJ reported to the new controller.

November one eight Mike Juliet, roger. Expect the visual approach to two-five left. India is current. Do you have the ATIS?" questioned the controller.

"Expect two-five left. Negative on the ATIS. I'll let you know when we have the numbers," responded MJ.

"I can give them to you if you want," offered the controller.

"That'll be fine," said MJ.

179

"Winds, one niner zero at ten. Sky clear, visibility unlimited. Altimeter, three zero point one five. Taxiway Gulf four and Foxtrot four closed until further notice. Landing and departing on runways two-five left, two-five right, and two-six."

"Altimeter point one five, one eight Mike Juliet," she repeated.

Otto sat down and began feeding information into the GPS. He had Totec intersection in the active mode and Phoenix International Airport stored in the database. He set the localizer frequency into both nav radios and set the omni-bearing selector to 258°, in alignment with the runway heading. The weather was great; they weren't going to have to shoot an approach. However, Otto and MJ liked to dial up the localizer on the landing runway just the same; it helped them make sure they were lined up with the correct one. This became especially helpful when landing at airports with multiple parallel runways, like Phoenix.

"OK, Cap, you're loaded and ready for bear," reported Otto. "Anything else I can do for you before we enter the fray?"

"No, thanks. Unless traffic gets especially heavy, this should be a piece of cake. Famous last words, eh Otto?" MJ said, as she turned and shot him that wide, shit-eating grin Otto knew so well.

"How's about letting me do the radio work? It would be nice to feel needed."

"Sure thing, Ottoman. Just don't go into that DJ mode with the Elvis overtones. These Phoenix guys don't have much of a sense of humor when it comes to breaking protocol. If you care to remember, I spent ten minutes on the phone with the shift supervisor the last time we came through here, getting my ass chewed about the need to do things expeditiously to keep the flow moving. Never mind that ours was the only plane they were handling at the time. That call for requests and dedications, along with the 'Thank-you-very-much, thank-you-very-much,' seemed to really put her over the edge. So let's not push anybody's buttons today, OK?"

"Ten-four, Good Buddy. Ah, I mean roger, wilco, over, and out," Otto said, between guffaws and attempted Elvis gyrations in his seat. "I was thinking of doing Walter Cronkite to keep it more professional, Boss. But I'll do it by the book, just for you."

"Much appreciated," she said.

"Douglas one eight Mike Juliet, Phoenix. Fly heading three six zero, descend and maintain four thousand five hundred."

"Three six zero, down to four thousand five hundred, and we have the airport in sight," Otto reported.

Otto had barely released the push-to-talk switch on the yoke when the controller came back with, "One eight Mike Juliet, contact Phoenix tower on one two six point eight."

"One two six point eight, one eight Juliet. Adios!" Otto responded.

MJ glared at Otto for the inappropriate remark.

Otto dialed up the tower frequency and keyed his mic. "Phoenix tower, Douglas One eight Mike Juliet inbound for two five left."

"One eight Mike Juliet, you are number two to land runway two-five left, 737 on base. Report traffic in sight. Caution, wake turbulence," the controller rattled off.

"Number two for two-five left. The 737 is in sight—kind of hard to miss it, actually—One eight Mike Juliet," Otto reported to the controller.

"Roger. Follow the traffic, cleared to land runway two-five left."

"Cleared to land, one eight Mike Juliet," Otto repeated.

Otto glanced over to MJ who was slowly reducing power on the big bird and adjusting the elevator trim. "That OK, Boss?" he said, with a smirk on his face.

"That'll do, Wise Guy," she said. "Although I'm not sure your opinion on the 737 was necessary."

"What opinion? I was making a statement of fact."

"Stow it. Let's get this bird on the ground. Open your window, Otto. It's getting pretty toasty in here," MJ said, sliding her small side window open. The hot Arizona air rushed into the cockpit, grabbed pieces of her sandy hair, and tossed them loosely about her head.

MJ watched the 737 descend through its final approach path and planned her descent to stay slightly above it to avoid the wing-tip vortices that could turn the DC-3 up on its wing. She brought the manifold pressure back to twenty inches, checked to make sure the mixture was out of auto-lean and into auto-rich, and called for gear down and flaps one quarter. Otto grabbed the gear lever, pulled it slightly away from him and then to the gear down position. While he waited for the gear to extend and lock, he grabbed the flap handle and moved it slightly away from him and down, until the flap indicator read one-quarter. When the gear-down hydraulic pressure dial equaled pressure on the main system indicator, he placed the gear lever in the neutral position. The single, green, gear-safe indicator light illuminated on the right side of the panel in front of him. He reached over and pushed the gear locking-lever to the floor and secured it with the latch. He then placed both of his feet on the brakes at the top of the rudder pedals and pushed. The hydraulic system pressure dropped slightly from fluid moving to the braking system and returned to normal when he released his feet from the pedals. He reached up and flipped the fuel boost pumps on for each engine and the switches for the landing lights. As a final check, he made sure that the tail wheel was locked. All of this was accomplished in less than a minute, as Otto's hands sped through the before landing procedures, something they had done so many times before.

"Gear down and locked, flaps a quarter, and pressure's good. Pumps on, lights on, tail wheel locked," he reported.

"Flaps two," requested MJ, as she continued to trim the elevator pressure on the heavy plane. It continued to slow and descend.

"Flaps a half," reported Otto, when the flap indicator showed that they had deployed halfway.

MJ had noted the touchdown point of the 737 and made a mental note of it. It will be easy enough to land just beyond that point, insuring no problems from wake turbulence, and still have a ton of runway to stop the DC-3 without wearing on the brake pads or the large balloon tires unnecessarily. She muscled the big bird from the base leg to final and lined up on the extended centerline of runway two-five left.

"Flaps three," she called over to Otto.

"Flaps three quarters," Otto responded, as he moved the flap lever out and down again and watched the flap indicator move to three-quarters.

MJ continued to trim little by little. She glanced at the airspeed settling around ninety knots, checked her distance to the runway, checked airspeed again, and called for full flaps.

"Flaps full," Otto reported.

The airspeed of the DC-3 dropped to eighty-five knots and remained there; the airplane was a very stable platform and liked to fly. Those big, broad wings gobbled up air molecules like a starving pilot in a popcorn feeding frenzy and would hold that bird steady as long as you pleased. MJ just rode her down the centerline as if she was on an imaginary slide. As the Doug passed over the threshold of two-five left, MJ began to pull back on the control wheel and reduce the throttles. What was once a steady roar of pure horsepower now became a gentle purring of idling cylinders, as MJ continued with the back pressure on the yoke and waited for the big tires to sing their touchdown song. A deep "churk, churk" resounded from underneath the DC-3 when the wheels made contact with the runway. MJ pushed forward

on the control wheel to keep the
bird on the ground and dump the
remaining lift being generated by
the wings.

"Flaps up," she called over to
Otto, who already had his hand on
the flap lever and pulled it up on
her command.

"Flaps coming up," he reported. He
moved the lever to the neutral
position when the flap indicator
read zero.

MJ waited until the airspeed
reached sixty knots and then began
pulling slowly back on the yoke,
flying the tail wheel gently to the
ground. There was the final "churk"
from the back of the plane when the
tail wheel made contact with the
surface. MJ began the mad dance on
the rudder pedals that kept the
airplane straight. Strong legs were
a requisite for driving the DC-3 on
the ground, and MJ had developed a
strong pair from many years of
flying her.

"Get the after stuff!" she yelled
over to Otto, as the plane slowed.

Otto reached up and turned off the fuel boost pumps and landing lights. He moved the cowl flap selector to "open" and looked out his window to confirm that they were. He asked MJ to confirm the cowl flaps on her side were open, then he moved the lever to "off," preventing lost pressure to the system.

"Where are you parking today?" asked the tower controller.

"We need to go to Mesa Air," Otto responded, as he finished his after landing duties.

"Roger. Taxi to Foxtrot-three, contact ground one three two point fifty-five.

"Thirty-two fifty-five," Otto repeated and dialed up the frequency in the standby window.

As MJ approached taxiway F-3, she unlocked the tail wheel. She turned right off the runway, crossed over the hold line, and stopped.

"Phoenix ground, Douglas one eight Mike Juliet at Foxtrot three. We'd like to go to Mesa Air, please,"

Otto requested of the new ATC controller.

"Douglas one eight Mike Juliet, roger. Turn right on Foxtrot to Foxtrot one-one, hold short two-five right, acknowledge hold short instructions."

"Right on Foxtrot to Foxtrot one-one, hold short twenty-five right," Otto repeated.

MJ taxied the DC-3 down the long taxiway to their holding point. The trip was longer than usual because they were unable to exit the runway at taxiway F four, which would have put them nearer to their destination. The controller cleared them to cross the end of runway two-five before they arrived, and MJ maneuvered the big airplane around the end of the runway and onto taxiway E eleven.

"One eight Mike Juliet. Mesa Air is at your twelve o'clock just behind the Customs building. You will be entering the non-visibility area and we will not be able to help you avoid other aircraft. You're on your own," the controller warned.

"Understood. Talk to you in a bit, one eight Mike Juliet."

Phoenix International is one of those large airports where the tower is located in such a place as to produce blind spots on the field. Although the ground controllers can see and control most traffic, these areas are particularly hazardous to pilots due to the lack of the extra pair of eyes controllers offer pilots when moving.

"Keep your eyes peeled, Otto, and make sure I clear everything by a country mile on your side," MJ ordered. She continued to maneuver the big plane toward the freight office.

"No problem, Cap. It looks pretty quiet down this end of the field, today," Otto assured her.

One of the line guys had emerged from Mesa Air and was waving his orange wands to get their attention. MJ watched as he positioned himself where he wanted her to put the nose of the airplane. He motioned the plane to make a big arc and waved it in toward him until he stood in front of, and slightly to the pilot's side of, the Gooney's nose. He motioned her forward, crossed the orange sticks into a big X when she reached the designated parking spot, and brought the plane to a stop. MJ moved the throttles until she had about one thousand rpms, grabbed the mixture levers on the console, and brought them both to the aft, idle/cutoff position. The big engines clunked and rattled to a stop. MJ reached up and turned off the magnetos, the radio master switch, and then the battery master. She had locked the tail wheel as the plane straightened and drifted its last few feet to parking.

Otto was up and out of his seat as soon as the plane came to a stop. He walked down the slanted fuselage to the tail of the plane, grabbed the chocks and control surface locks, and threw them over by the ladder. He opened one of the freight doors and squinted at the bright Arizona landscape, as the hot dry wind of the Arizona desert met him head on. He felt like he had just opened the oven in his mother's kitchen to check on the pies for Thanksgiving.

"Key-rye-iced!" he shouted, as he backed away from the door. "How the hell does anyone live around here?"

"Air-conditioning," responded the lineman, poking his head into the cargo door of the airplane. "You go from your air-conditioned house to your air-conditioned car to your air-conditioned job . . . this one excluded. If it weren't for air-conditioning, the only thing living in this part of the world would be rattlesnakes and lizards, and they would only come out when the sun was down. Hand me your chocks, and I'll get the wheels for you."

"Thanks," Otto said, tossing the large, rubber chock blocks to the edge of the door. "They say this dry heat isn't as bad as the humid areas, but I don't see any benefits. This sucks!"

"You get used to it when you're out in it everyday. You need any fuel?"

"Yeah, top it off. We've got a long haul," Otto answered.

"Everything inside is air-conditioned," the lineman offered. "Just make sure to drink plenty of water. You won't even know you're dehydrated until it's too late and you start feeling ill. It wouldn't hurt to take salt tablets, either. We have them inside; they're free, so help yourself."

"Thanks, Man. I think I'll just plant my sorry ass in front of the TV in that air-conditioned lounge until my captain tells me it's time to go and the engines are up and running," Otto said.

Otto put the ladder in place and climbed down onto the baking blacktop. He reached back inside the airplane and grabbed the surface control locks for the elevator, rudder, and ailerons. It wasn't very windy, but he knew that this place could blow up a gale in very short order. Besides, he didn't have any idea just how long they would be here. Waiting for freight was the bane of the freight dog. The only good that ever came of the waiting game was a chance to sleep and a chance to eat something other than the same crummy pilot food found in

FBO vending machines from sea to shining sea.

"If McDonald's could figure a way to get a quarter-pounder with cheese and fries into a vending machine, that would be something," he mused.

"I'm going to check on the freight, Otto. You give the customer a call and tell them we've landed at Phoenix. We'll call them again when we know what time we'll be airborne."

"Roger that, MJ," he said. Otto closed up the cargo doors of the Doug and headed for the cool, refreshing oasis of the pilot's lounge in the FBO. His shirt was sweat-soaked before he had walked twenty yards.

"Dry heat, my ass. This sucks!"

THIRTEEN

Otto Archibald Sanderson walked through the doors of the FBO and into an oasis of cool air. He waved at the girls behind the desk and headed for the men's room—always the first stop for every pilot deplaning—relieved himself, washed his hands and face, and checked himself in the mirror. He had some color on his round smooth face; the Texas sun was quick in its work and his complexion was light, making him more susceptible to burning. His deep, dark brown eyes looked back at him from the reflection and followed his hands as they moved over his face and through his hair. He stepped back to get a better look at his midsection. Although he did a lot of sitting, ate a lot of junk food, and drank his share of beer, he thought he was looking pretty good. "Sure, I could lose ten or fifteen pounds," he thought, "but at least I ain't got a gut hanging over my belt. Not yet anyway."

Inspection complete, he proclaimed himself good-looking, a bit tired, and fit for duty. He checked his head for any gray strands that may have woven themselves into his inky black hair since the last inspection. Although he had a couple of years to go before reaching the unbearable age of thirty-five, he was afraid he was going to be prematurely gray like his dad. His father always reminded him that it made one look distinguished—a title Otto was in no hurry to have applied to him. Gray was gray; it made you look old. That's the way he looked at it. He wasn't ready for the rocker, just yet. There were ladies waiting for the Ottoman, and if he ever stayed in one place long enough, he was going to make himself available to them.

197

Otto walked back into the common area and looked for the pilots' lounge. A sign on the wall directed him down the hall and past the vending machines to a comfortable room with a TV, couch, and two reclining chairs. There was a small library of videos stored alphabetically on two shelves next to the TV. Otto strolled over and walked his fingers across a few of the titles. All of them had something to do with flying; a few were full-length movies about W.W.II. He counted six titles with John Wayne. "The Duke," he thought. "Someone's a fan."

He pulled Air America from the shelf and put it into the VCR. He had seen this film a number of times; he even had his own copy. Mel Gibson was one of his favorite actors, and he enjoyed Robert Downing Jr. in this movie, as well. He decided it wouldn't hurt to watch it again. Besides, if the freight should arrive in the middle of it, it was no great loss; he knew how it came out. He adjusted the volume, plunked himself down in one of the easy chairs, pushed it back into a reclining position, put the remote down on the table next to him, and immediately fell asleep.

Otto was an Air Force brat. His father, Major Robert "Rob" Sanderson, was a career flyer, and they had traveled all over the globe. Otto had spent parts of his childhood in Germany, Italy, Japan, Okinawa, Hawaii, and California. By the time he reached his mid-teens, the re-assignments had become fewer and fewer until the family made their final move to McGuire Air Force Base just outside Fort Dix. Although the base offered a stable environment for Otto and his mother, his dad was often required to fly overseas and was away from home a great deal. Otto missed him when he was gone, but he didn't miss all of the moving they had to endure over the years.

Otto started flying at an early age; his father would take him up every chance he got. The stability of a permanent duty station in New Jersey gave Otto the opportunity to take lessons and work toward his pilot's license. He waited until he was just a few months shy of his seventeenth birthday (the legal age requirement to be licensed by the FAA) to get an instructor and begin building the hours to fulfill the requirements of the certificate. He already knew how to fly; he had been doing it since he was ten. This was more of a formality than anything else. He had passed his written exam with a perfect score and mastered the airplane before he ever gave an instructor a dime. The lessons went quickly and smoothly. Otto had his private pilot certificate just three days after celebrating his seventeenth birthday.

He thought he was going to follow in his father's footsteps and be an Air Force pilot; however, he didn't have his father's eyes and couldn't meet the stringent vision requirements of the Air Force. But he loved to fly and wanted to fly, so he wasn't going to let this obstacle get in the way. He joined the Air Force anyway after completing high school and signed on to be a load-master for the big C-130s and giant C-5s. He joined the base's flying club and continued to build his flying time and experience wherever he was stationed. By the time he completed his four years of duty he had earned his instrument, commercial, and multiengine certificates and logged two thousand hours of flight time, three hundred of which were multiengine.

After leaving the Air Force, Otto worked for a variety of small, Part 135 charter-for-hire companies. Mostly he flew on the eastern seaboard. Occasionally he caught a trip that took him to Cleveland, Chicago, Cincinnati, and a few places down South. He loved these trips; they added a new dimension to flight planning and weather-related problems. His goal was to build flight time enough so that he could fly a commuter route for one of the major airlines and eventually move up to the coveted right seat of a commercial jet. Unfortunately, Otto had failed to consider one factor in his planning . . . a college degree. He ran into this reality when he went for his first interview with one of the regional carriers. They were happy to hire him, and he could even make captain someday, but he wouldn't be able to go any further with his flying career until he earned a degree. They suggested he use the GI Bill to take courses while flying the commuters for them, but Otto was a pilot not a bookworm. He began to look at the downside of flying for the major airlines until he talked himself right out of it. "Bus drivers," he called them. The real flying, he thought, was charter: anytime, anywhere, through any kind of weather. And you didn't have to wear a tie. He branded himself "Freight Dog" and told the majors to take a hike.

Otto took a job flying DC-3s around the New England area for a while, then moved to the Caribbean to fly DC-3s on island hops. He took a short hiatus from this job to ferry DC-3s from different countries in Central America to outfits in the US, which were overhauling them and selling them to freight companies. Some of them went back to the countries they came from, so Otto became a recognizable figure to many an army officer in countries like El Salvador, Nicaragua, Panama, and Columbia. He also discovered he had a natural propensity for the language. He often had to lay over for days and sometimes weeks to teach foreign pilots about the airplane. This gave him plenty of opportunity to learn Spanish, and he became very good at it.

Although admitting he wasn't much for books, Otto began to see the limitations of his chosen career. He loved aviation and he loved to fly; however, he decided something extra was needed to ensure a solid career. He went back to work for a charter company in New Jersey and worked out a deal that would give him sufficient time to go to school and earn an airframe and power plant certificate. He would be a mechanic. It was good money, he would never be without a job, he would be employable everywhere. Flying the regular runs for the company gave him a predictable schedule and sufficient downtime to pursue the courses. He figured if the flying opportunities were few and far between, he could spend his time working in the hangar.

It took him a couple of years, but he completed the courses, took the tests, and became certified. Unfortunately, his flying opportunities had diminished during this time, and he soon became restless and moved on. He returned to the outfit that was moving DC-3s around the America's and spent his non-flying time learning the in's and out's of the big Gooney Birds. They were one of a kind.

"Oh, Archibald," a voice deep and far away said.

"Archie," he heard again.

"Otto Archibald 'Archie' Sanderson," he heard, as the mist of unfulfilled sleep began to lift.

Otto heard a faint whisper next to his ear: "Archibald Sanderson," it said. "Your captain is calling you back from the depths of hell. Release those vixens, turn your back on Satan, resist the vices of evil, and return to me, for I will take you to the heavens and show you the glory of the angels. Arise, Archibald! Arise!"

MJ jumped back from Otto's chair just as he snapped his head around and reached out to grab her. Trying to get up, he fell out of the lounge chair and crawled after her. He found his footing for a moment and then tripped and fell back to the floor. He rolled over on his back and looked up into MJ's face. She stood over him, laughing.

"Two can play at this game, eh, Ottoman?" she said.

Otto gritted his teeth and spit back, "How many times do I have to tell you, Miss Mary Jane Carlson, to never, and I mean NEVER, EVER, call me Archibald, or Archie, or anything even close to that NAME!"

"Oh c'mon, Otto. No one heard me. I was whispering it right into your ear. Now you, of course, have just broadcast that aristocratic, *nom de famille* to the entire FBO. I bet those two beauties at the front desk are just *dying* to meet their royal guest."

"*You* are a royal shit, MJ. You better have a good reason for waking me up."

"Of course I do. The freight is going to be late. It seems that the truck broke down somewhere in Mexico, and it will be at least four hours before they get here. I

205

thought you would like to have this little tidbit of information to better plan your day."

"Four hours! Otto exclaimed. "Four hours! Key-Riced! We'll never get to Chicago at this rate."

"Well, the good news is that we get paid for down-time on this run. The bad news is that the company waiting for the freight in Chicago is pissed. But the other good news is that it's not our fault, so they're not pissed at us. Don't you just love this business?"

"So you woke me up to tell me I can sleep for another four hours?" he asked.

"Well, that *is* an option, I suppose. However, they have a courtesy car here; I thought you might like to join me for some authentic Southwestern chow. It beats the vending buffet."

"*Anything* beats the vending buffet. Sure, I'll go. We should stop and stock up on bottled water, too. We're getting pretty low."

"No problem. Meet me at the front desk in about ten minutes. I have to make a few more calls, and then we can be on our way."

"You got it. See you in ten."

"Bye, Archieeee", she threw over her shoulder to him, as she walked out of the lounge.

"You'd better hope you never fall asleep again in your life, Mary Jane Carlson, or you just might not wake up!" he shot back.

MJ stuck her head back into the lounge, "Is that any way to talk to your captain, Mr. First Officer? Whatever happened to that military discipline Uncle Sam spent so much time cultivating in you?"

"Cultivate this!" he said, and threw the empty video box at her.

FOURTEEN

Route 2, the United States of Mexico, somewhere between Tajitos and Nogales.

"Ay, chingada! Slow down, Guillermo! You're gonna get us killed," Ricardo said, bracing himself with his hands against the ceiling of the cab to keep from banging his head. "These roads are too dangerous to go this fast, and there are too many holes. You're going to bust the axle."

"You sound like an old woman, Amigo," Guillermo said. "You know

208

that I am the best driver in all of Mexico. Nothing is going to happen. Besides, we're late. You took too long for your lunch, Pendejo; now we have to make it up."

"We're not *that* late, Cabrón," Ricardo came back. "What about the freight? You're going to break it."

"You're going to break my cojones if you don't shut up," Guillermo said, dodging a large hole in the road. "Maybe you should ride with the freight, just to make sure that I don't break any of it."

"Ain't gonna happen. Maybe you should let me drive."

"No way. You're just along to help with the freight. You're not going to drive anything."

"What's this?" Ricardo asked, squinting at an object ahead.

"Ay, chingada! It looks like someone broke down. Man, I wouldn't want to be stuck way out here in the middle of nowhere."

"Do you have a cell phone with you?" Ricardo asked.

"No. I dropped it a couple of days ago, and it hasn't worked since."

"What's he got on his head?"

"I can't tell; we're too far away. Probably a hat; the sun is dangerous out here."

"We should stop and see if they need anything," Ricardo offered. "We can at least leave them some water and send help from Nogales."

"We're running late, Bro," Guillermo answered.

"Hey, Cabrón. That could be *you* out there. Wouldn't you want someone to stop and help?"

"Chingada," Guillermo spat. "Man, we're never going to get this stuff to Phoenix. OK, fine! We'll stop to see if they need water and tell them we'll send help from Nogales, but we can't offer them a ride; there's no room."

Reluctantly, Guillermo downshifted and slowed the truck. He pulled up behind the car parked on the side of the road.

"Hey man, look!" Ricardo said. "These guys are ragheads. What are *they* doing out here?"

"Ragheads?" Guillermo asked. "What the hell are ragheads?"

"You know, Arabs. They wear turbans, rags, on their heads."

"Man, they're a long way from home. Maybe they were out here looking for oil or something," Guillermo offered. "Let's see what they need."

Ricardo and Guillermo got out of the truck and approached the man standing outside the car. He was wearing traditional Arab garb: a long robe and head cover. The other occupant remained seated in the driver's seat of the car.

"Buenas tardes, Amigo," Guillermo said.

"Buenas tardes," the man answered. "I'm sorry, but that's about the extent of my Spanish. I hope you speak some English."

"Chingada. I speak English all the time. Everyone in Mexico speaks English," Guillermo answered. "What happened to your car?"

"I don't know. We were driving along and it just stopped running. American cars; they are not so dependable. I'll take a Mercedes anytime."

"A Mercedes?" Guillermo said, with eyes wide open. "Chingada, Amigo, that's a lot of money."

"Yes, I suppose so. Can you give us a lift?"

"No, I'm sorry. We don't have any room and we're running behind schedule. We can give you some water, if you need it, and send help from Nogales. It will only take a couple of hours for someone to come out and get you."

"That's too bad," the man said. "We're running behind schedule, as well."

The man turned as if to return to the car, then spun around to face Guillermo and Ricardo. Two shots rang out; Guillermo fell to the road. Ricardo watched his partner go down, turned, and ran back toward the truck. Another shot resounded, and Ricardo felt his right leg give out. He stumbled, caught himself on the bumper of the truck, and limped toward the driver's side door. He turned and saw the man approach, holding a pistol by his side. Ricardo reached for the cab door; the man raised the pistol and took aim. The next shot caught Ricardo in the left side and dropped him to the pavement. Ricardo struggled to breathe, as blood soaked his shirt and began to spread onto the road. The man raised the pistol and aimed at Ricardo's head.

"Ramón, enough!" said the man who had been sitting in the car. "He will die soon enough; you don't have to waste bullets on him. You have made enough noise already. Throw them into the trunk, and let's get out of here. We still have much to do."

Ramón looked at Ricardo and returned his pistol to the holster under his robe. He dragged Ricardo over to the car, where he and Rafael placed the dying man into the trunk. They walked over to Guillermo, picked him up, and threw him on top of Ricardo.

"Take the truck to the transfer point," Rafael said. "I will meet you there after I dispose of the bodies. Be quick about it; we must do this quickly and get the shipment to Phoenix as soon as possible."

Ramón climbed into the cab and turned the key. The engine caught immediately. He waited until Rafael pulled away in the car, put the gearshift into first, released the clutch, and pulled out onto the highway. About two miles down the road, he turned the truck off onto an obscure dirt road and headed east. Twenty minutes later, he pulled into the yard of a deserted ranch and drove around behind a dilapidated barn. He got down out of the truck and went inside, removed

the turban and robe, and stuffed
them under some bales of old moldy
hay stacked in one of the stalls. He
returned to the back of the truck
and broke the seal of the lock on
the cargo door. He cut the lock with
bolt cutters brought from the barn.
Opening the door, he climbed inside
and removed the freight, dumping it
directly behind the truck. When the
truck was empty, he drove around to
the front of the deserted house and
backed it up to the porch. He placed
two, two-by-six planks from the back
of the truck onto the porch and
brought three pallets from the house
and placed them inside the truck. He
grabbed a dolly and moved canisters
from the living room to the porch,
into the back of the truck, and onto
the pallets. When he had both
pallets loaded, he got a roll of
metal strapping and strapped the
containers together on each pallet.
Satisfied the load was secure, he
removed the planks from the truck,
rolled the door down, and secured it
with a replacement lock. He pulled a
new seal from a manila envelope—it
was identical to the one he had
removed—and threaded it through the
two rings that held the door lock.
He took a clamping tool from his

back pocket and locked the seal in place. Ramón climbed into the cab and checked the bill-of-lading. He pulled a piece of paper from his shirt pocket and compared the number to the tare of the freight the Mexicans had been hauling. "Close enough," he said. He tossed the paperwork onto the seat beside him and dug a cigarette out of his shirt pocket. He lit the unfiltered cigarette, pulled on it, took a deep breath, and exhaled, letting the smoke from his lungs explode on the windshield and escape through the open side windows. "That was the easy part," he said to himself. "Now things will get interesting."

Ramón finished his cigarette and turned to look down the dusty road. A vehicle was approaching rapidly, trailing a plume of dust behind it. He got out of the truck, checked his pistol, and hid just inside the doorway of the house. As the dust cloud got closer, Ramón could make out the car in front of it; it was Rafael. He placed his pistol back into its holster and pulled his shirt over it.

Rafael pulled into the yard and drove the car directly into the barn. He got out of the car, removed the rubber gloves and Arab garb he was wearing, took a leak in the corner, and strolled out to the truck.

"We all set?" he asked Ramón.

"Yeah. We're set."

"Ramón, do you still have your pistol on you?" he asked.

"Of course. Why wouldn't I?"

"Well, I can think of two reasons: one, you just killed two people with that pistol; it's the murder weapon. Two, we have to cross the border, and the border people frown on Hispanics with pistolas. What do you think?"

"So what am I supposed to do, just throw it away?" Ramón asked.

"My thought exactly. Why don't you put it with that costume you were wearing? Maybe the authorities will believe it belongs to an Arab. You can get another one in the States;

217

everybody has guns in the United States. No problem!"

Ramón pulled the pistol from the holster and looked it over. He placed it in his shirt and rubbed it down, removing any chance his fingerprints would remain. He walked back into the barn and over to the pile of hay that covered the robe and turban. He lifted the hay with his boot, tossed the pistol in with the other items, and returned to the truck. Rafael had already started the engine. He put it in gear as soon as Ramón was on board.

"On to Nogales, Amigo," Rafael said. "Let's hope the border guards are sleepy and stupid today."

"And if they're not?" asked Ramón.

"If they're not? Well then, I guess we will have a nice long vacation with free room and board at the expense of the American taxpayer," Rafael laughed. "Don't worry, Amigo; we have friends in high places." Rafael looked over at Ramón and winked.

FIFTEEN

"There's the border," Rafael said. "Light a cigarette for me."

Ramón took a cigarette from the pack in his shirt pocket, lit it, and passed it to Rafael. Rafael put it into the corner of his mouth and let it smolder there. He downshifted and slowed the truck as they approached the Mexican side of the crossing. Reading the name on the side of the truck, the guard waved him on. He shifted into second gear, waved at the guard, and drove the 100 yards to the American checkpoint.

"Papers, please," the American border guard asked.

Ramón passed a small stack of papers to Rafael who passed them to the border guard.

"What are you hauling?" the guard asked Rafael.

"Car parts, I think," he answered.

"You think?" asked the guard.

"Well, officer, the truck was locked and sealed when I left Tajitos, and the bill-of-lading lists a bunch of things I think belong on cars," Rafael said. "I haven't seen them with my own eyes, though. So I can only think that I'm carrying car parts, can't I?"

"Where are you taking them?" asked the guard.

"To Phoenix," replied Rafael.

"Where in Phoenix?"

"To the airport. The name of the company is there on the papers."

"Wait here," the guard commanded.

Rafael looked at Ramón and shrugged. He watched the guard in the side-view mirror as he walked around to the back of the truck. The guard appeared on the other side and walked up to Ramón's window.

"You aren't the guys who normally make this trip, are you?" he asked Ramón.

"No, Señor," replied Ramón.

"Where are they?"

"They got fired," Rafael said, leaning over toward Ramón's window.

"Fired? For what?"

"The boss caught them trying to smuggle some wetbacks with one of the shipments. I guess they figured that they wouldn't be stopped, because they were well known at the crossings. They probably thought they could get away with it, one time, and make some extra money. It was a night run. Unfortunately for them, the boss stopped by the plant

221

on the way home from a big party to see how things were going. He arrived just when the people were getting into the back of the truck. He fired them both on the spot."

"How long have you two been working for the company?" the guard asked.

"Just a couple of weeks," Rafael answered.

"I thought so. I haven't seen you two before," he said.

"That's a coincidence. I haven't seen you before, either," Rafael smiled at the guard and blew some smoke in his direction.

Ramón glared at Rafael and removed a cigarette from his pocket.

The guard went into the guardhouse and brought out a mirror with a long handle. He placed it under the truck and slowly walked around the vehicle, checking for anything that looked unusual or out of place. Another guard came out of the main building and started walking toward the truck. Ramón looked at Rafael with questioning eyes. Rafael shrugged his shoulders and put the cigarette out in the ashtray.

"Hey, Mike. What are you doing?" asked the man approaching the truck.

"I'm checking the undercarriage; what do you think I'm doing?"

"C'mon, let's get going. There's a line building behind them. These guys come through here all the time. They're clean. That company can't afford to get busted; it would cost them too damn much."

"Yeah, well, the company might be clean, but these guys have only been working for them for a couple of weeks. You can't be too careful these days, John."

"Would you like me to call the company and check these guys out?" John offered.

Ramón and Rafael looked at each other. Mike looked at both of them then back to John.

"Hey, you're the boss. If you say they're OK, then that's just fine

with me. It's your ass, not mine,"
Mike answered.

"That's right, it is. And I've got
plenty of it," John said, as he
slapped himself on the butt. "Let's
go, you guys. Get moving. Now, if
you were Arabs . . . well . . . hey,
I'd have you out here on the street,
buck naked, looking into every one
of your creases and crevasses with
the sharpest thing I could find. But
seeing as how you're Mexicans,
shoot, you wouldn't have the get-up-
and-go to be tourists let alone
terrorists. Get out of here!"

Mike moved away from the truck and
John motioned them to continue. As
they pulled away, John tipped his
hat to Rafael and gave him just a
hint of a smile.

"Assholes," Ramón said.

"I wonder why they've got it in
for the Mexicans?" Rafael asked.

"Do I really look like a Mexican?"
asked Ramón.

"It must be the mustache," offered
Rafael. "Apparently, we both do. At

least to those two. It's a good thing, too." Rafael looked at Ramón and winked. "On to Tucson, Casa Grande, then Phoenix, and we're home free. That wasn't so bad now, was it?"

"It seems to me you were trying to piss that guy off," Ramón said. "What was with the wisecrack about not seeing him before?"

"Nervous people don't make jokes at authority figures. They just say, 'Yes, Sir;' 'No, Sir;' 'Anything you say, Sir.' I figure if I'm a wise-ass, nobody's going to think I'm hiding something. Besides, it's fun. Don't you like to have fun, Ramón?"

"I don't think going to jail is having fun, Rafael."

"Are we going to jail? Is that where we are going? I don't think so, Ramón. We are going to Phoenix. Phoenix, Arizona. Gee haw! He looked at Ramón and grinned, "Give Mesa Air a call, Amigo. Let them know we're running late."

SIXTEEN

"Well that was certainly different," Otto said, as they pulled away from the Lone Cactus Grill.

"It's like I told you, Ottoman. There is life after Taco Bell; a better life at that."

"I've got to hand it to you, MJ. I've never had steak strips as tender as those, and that sauce, man, how do they think that stuff up?"

"Years and years of experimenting and combining recipes, I guess," she answered. Next time we're in Phoenix, remind me to take you to Juanito's Corral. We'll get a couple of orders of his carnitas. Now *that's* something that'll blow you away; I guaran-damn-tee it, fer sure," MJ said, slipping into a West Texas drawl and tipping her hat in Otto's direction.

"Can't wait. If it's half as good as that dish I just devoured, I won't be disappointed."

MJ reached over and patted his belly. "I don't think you'll have that much trouble waiting. This spare tire you're carrying looks like it will supply *all* your nutritional needs until we get back to Phoenix."

"Always room for more, Cap. Always room for more," he said, patting his belly.

"I better do a new weight and balance before we take off," MJ kidded. "We might have to off-load some fuel, Otto. Did you have to eat so much?"

"Have to? No! Want to? Didn't plan on it, but I just couldn't resist. I've never had anything that tasted that good before."

Well next time, Pard, I'm only paying for *one* meal at a sitting. You are, literally, eating up the profits."

"Give it a rest, MJ. Who bought the sandwiches back in El Paso? And how about dinner last night?"

"How about dinner last night?" she asked. "I bet my soup and salad just about broke your little piggy bank, didn't it?"

"I'm going to start keeping a ledger," he said. "I bet I spend a good deal more of my wages on our meals than you do."

"Do it!" she urged. "We'll check it at the end of the month and then settle the difference. I could use a little extra cash."

We'll see," he said. "Look, there. That looks like our freight."

"I believe you're right, Sir. It's about time, too. You take care of getting it on board, and I'll go file a flight plan and get a briefing."

MJ pulled into the reserved parking space at Mesa Air and went inside. She returned the keys to the girl at the desk and headed for the pilot briefing room. Otto walked over to the truck but was unable to locate the driver, so he went inside the FBO and asked the receptionist if she had seen him.

"Those two guys over there," she said. They arrived about ten minutes ago."

"Thanks."

Otto went over to the two men watching the local news on the television.

"Hey, guys. You the ones with that truck out there?"

"Yes," Rafael spoke first. "Are you the pilot?"

"One of them. Back up to the cargo doors of the DC-3 over there."

"What's a DC-3?" Rafael asked.

"That big, ugly, olive-drab monster out there, sitting all by itself. It's so ugly no other planes will go near it," Otto told them, laughing at his own joke.

Rafael stood up and looked to where Otto was pointing.

"I don't think she is so ugly," Rafael said. "I think that she just needs a new paint job, that's all. C'mon, Ramón. It's time to go to work."

Ramón climbed out of the easy chair and looked over at Otto. Otto met his gaze and got a sick feeling in his gut. He quickly looked away and headed for the door.

"I'll meet you at the plane."

Otto had them stop the truck a few feet from the cargo doors. He took the papers from Rafael, looked through them, and went to the back of the truck to check the seal. He compared the numbers on the seal with the numbers on the bill-of-lading and then looked at the tare for the freight.

"OK," he said. "Everything looks good. Let's get it on board."

Ramón cut the seal and opened the lock. He rolled up the door and climbed into the truck. Otto stuck his head in to get a look at how the freight was packed.

"They're on skids?" he asked Ramón.

"Yes," Ramón answered. "Do you want me to cut the bands so we can load them individually?" he asked Otto.

"No. No, don't do that. Let me see if I can get a forklift from this place," he answered. "Wait here. This shouldn't take long."

Otto walked back to the FBO and went inside. Rafael and Ramón climbed back into the cab of the truck and turned on the air-conditioning. It was too hot to be hanging around on the blacktop waiting. Otto emerged from the FBO and looked toward the hangars. A man riding a forklift emerged from the one closest to the FBO and headed toward the plane. Otto and the forklift arrived at the same time. Ramón climbed out of the passenger side of the truck and approached Otto.

"Have him pull up about twenty feet," Otto said to him.

Ramón walked around to the driver's side of the truck and spoke to Rafael. The truck pulled up, and Otto directed the forklift driver to place the pallet just inside the cargo door. Otto ran the winch cable underneath the freight pallets already on board, and then under the pallet that was just loaded into the doorway. He pushed the edge of the pallet around until it was square to the rest of the load, then attached the hook at the end of the cable to a ring on the 4 x 4 aligned with the back of the skid. He walked up to the outside of the cabin to the winch controls and threw the switch that activated the electric motor. The 4 x 4 tightened against the back of the skid, and the winch groaned as it dragged the skid across the metal floor and up against the last skid of the first load. Otto reversed the motor on the winch and slackened the cable. He unhooked the cable from the 4 x 4 and pulled it further down the fuselage, returned to the winch motor, let out some more slack, and pulled the cable far enough back to allow for the next skid. Ramón and Rafael had slid the other skid to the back of the truck, and the forklift driver had picked it up and brought it over to the plane, resting it on the ground as he waited.

"OK," Otto said. "Bring that one up."

The forklift driver lifted the load and gently placed it inside the airplane. Otto watched the sides and top of the load to make sure that they didn't strike any part of the fuselage. The driver put the load down on the floor, dropped the forks, pulled back a bit, and then lifted the load and shoved it further onto the plane.

"That's good," Otto said, as he held up his hand motioning the driver to stop.

The forklift driver lowered the forks of the lift and backed out from underneath the pallet. Otto hooked up the cable to the 4 x 4, again, and brought the load up against the others. He repeated the process once more and then released the cable, tossed the 4 x 4 into the back of the plane, wound the cable all the way back to the winch, and secured the load with straps. Otto climbed down out of the plane and picked up the paperwork that was lying on the ground secured to a clipboard. He signed the lading, took two copies for himself, and returned the rest to Rafael.

"Where do you go from here?" Rafael asked.

"Kansas City. A fuel stop," Otto answered.

"And then?" Rafael pressed.

"On to Chicago, weather permitting. Those are funny looking

containers," Otto offered to no one in particular.

"Probably hubcaps," Rafael said. "They're always looking for new ways to ship them. They're so cheap; they damage easily. Maybe they took a lesson from Pringles potato chips."

"Could be," Otto said. "I wish they were a little more specific on the product descriptions in these forms, though. I'd like to know just what I'm hauling around these friendly skies."

"Maybe you should talk to someone at the plant," offered Rafael.

"It wouldn't do any good. They do things just the way they want; you can't tell them anything. If you do complain, they just get someone else to haul their stuff. I guess I should be thankful that they seal the loads at the plant. At least we know it came from a reliable source. You start hauling for middlemen and you start asking for trouble. They could put anything in these things."

Rafael looked at Ramón and then back to Otto.

"That's right, Amigo. At least you know where this load came from, right?"

"That's right." He looked at Ramón, who hadn't said anything during the entire loading process. He felt a tug on his insides and a chill penetrating his whole being. Ramón just stared right through him. He looked back at Rafael.

"Your friend isn't much for conversation, is he?" he said.

"He thinks many things are better left unsaid; so he doesn't say much," Rafael said, grinning. "It's OK with me. I'd rather listen to CDs than to Ramón, any day," Rafael said, slapping Ramón lightly on the shoulder.

Ramón said something to Rafael in Spanish and climbed into the cab.

"Time to go, Amigo," Rafael said. "You have a safe flight. Maybe we'll see you again, OK?"

"Yeah, thanks," Otto replied. "See ya."

Otto watched the truck pull away and head for the gate. As it passed the FBO, Otto's gaze switched to the door of the building and MJ, walking toward the Gooney. He threw the paperwork into the back of the plane and began the preflight ritual he had done so many times before.

"All loaded? Got the paperwork, Ottoman?" MJ asked, as she pulled the safety pins from the gear locking levers.

"Yeah, Boss. We're loaded for bear and she's chompin' at the bit."

"Those two guys were a trip, weren't they?" she said. "Where were they from? They certainly didn't look like Mexicans to me."

"I don't know. They drove up from Mexico, but I don't think they're Mexicans, either. The one I spoke to didn't sound like a Mexican, and the other one didn't say a word; he just gave me the creeps."

"You've been watching too many movies."

"Maybe. But let's not forget what happened on September 11th in 2001, shall we? A little paranoia these days might be just what the doctor ordered."

"If my memory serves me right, most of those guys were Saudis. You know, Arabs. They weren't Mexicans, or whatever nationality those guys are," MJ said. "I can appreciate the need for caution, but I don't want to get so paranoid that I start looking at everyone of color with suspicion. If I did, we wouldn't be putting anything on this bird and carrying it aloft . . . without opening it first."

"Speaking of opening," Otto said, take a look at the canisters on the pallets. Did you ever see anything packed like those?"

MJ poked her head in through the cargo doors and looked over the newly loaded freight.

"No. Can't say that I have. What did the paperwork say?"

"Auto parts."

"Mmmm. Could be anything, I suppose. Was the truck sealed when it arrived?"

"Yes. The driver thought they might be hubcaps."

"Well, if the truck was sealed, we know that whatever's in them must have come from the plant—our customer. They tell us they want this stuff in Chicago; we take this stuff to Chicago. The paperwork in order?" she asked.

"Yes, everything was the way it's supposed to be," he answered. "Those two guys just made me nervous, especially the one who wasn't driving. Every time he looked at me, it was if he was looking right through me—like I didn't exist, or something."

"Like I said, Ottoman. You watch too many movies. Let's get inside; I have some bad news for you."

239

SEVENTEEN

MJ climbed in first and made her way to the cockpit. Otto closed and latched the cargo doors and made his way up to the front of the plane. It was his leg to drive, so he took the left seat.

"What's up?" he asked.

"Weather," she said.

"How bad?" he asked.

"Fours and fives," she reported, referring to the thunderstorm rating system devised by the National

Weather Service: a "one" was small and innocuous. The storms increased in intensity and ferocity with each higher number.

"Great. And we'll be doing them at night, too, right?" he asked.

"Looks that way."

"Maybe you'd better give me the whole picture, Boss," he said.

"Along most of our route, these thunderstorms are widely scattered; we can probably avoid most of them without deviating too far. However, as our good fortune would have it, they are expecting major cells over and around Kansas City just about the time we arrive. We could be in for a rough ride if we decide to try an approach. Is the freight secure?" she asked.

"Very!"

"Good. We don't need to be ducking missiles while we're looking for a runway at minimums," she said. "If we had gotten out of here earlier, we probably could have avoided them altogether. But here we are, thanks to our Mexican Express friends."

"Not to worry, MJ. This old Night-Train loves thunderstorms. They are a Gooney Bird's delight, don't ya know."

"Yeah, right, Otto. You seem to have this habit of forgetting just how much fun it is up there flying through those things. Do you still have that egg on your head you collected on the last fly-through?"

"Caught me by surprise," he said. "You had the wheel to hold onto. If I hadn't been tuning radios for you just at that moment, I would've been able to hold on and not play pinball with my head. And, no, I don't have a knot there anymore."

"Poor Baby," she said, and patted him on the head. "This time, you have the wheel. So no excuses. And by the way, don't hesitate to ask for assistance should things get a little too dicey up there."

"Who knows?" he said. "Maybe we'll get lucky for once and all the boomers will have gone merrily on

their way east by the time we get
there."

"Yeah. Who knows?" MJ said. "Maybe
they'll be bowling in tornado alley
tonight, too. Time to crank'em."

Otto started the engines while MJ
called for their clearance to Kansas
City. After reading the clearance
back to clearance delivery, she
dialed up the ground controller, who
cleared them to the active runway,
with a reminder that they were on
their own until they were clear of
the tower's blind spot. It would be
dark in a couple of hours, but at
least part of this trip would be in
daylight. They would be able to see
what kind of trouble loomed in front
of them and go around it, if they
chose to. After that, they would
have to rely on ATC for storm
advisories, a scenario that didn't
always bring the best results. The
tower cleared them for a straight-
out departure, and Otto advanced the
throttles to start them on their
way. Thunderheads loomed on the not-
too-distant horizon, back-lit by the
setting sun.

EIGHTEEN

"Mary Jane, you'd better get up here, now!" Otto yelled over his shoulder. "Are you up?"

"I'm up! I'm up!" she yelled, sitting up on the futon and holding on to a tie-down strap with one hand and the side of the fuselage with the other.

They were five hours into their flight from Phoenix to Kansas City; it was dark, and they were running into heavier weather by the hour. The latest incursion was the worst, and the plane was being shaken *and* stirred. Otto was no longer able to hold altitude and was fighting to keep the wings level. He had requested and received a block clearance from ATC; the airspace between six and eight thousand feet was now his. MJ made her way to her seat and strapped herself in, pulling the seatbelt tighter than normal.

"What's up?" she asked.

"So far, we still are," he answered. "They thought they were giving us vectors around this mother, but I'm beginning to have my doubts."

The plane descended a thousand feet and then immediately lurched back to its original altitude. The temporary zero Gs in the cabin floated pencils and papers, but gravity quickly redistributed them during the ascent. Lightning flashed, and the resounding roar of the thunder shook the plane.

"Man," Otto said, "I felt that one in my boots."

"Are we with Kansas City Center, yet?" MJ asked.

"I don't think we're in Kansas at all, Toto," he answered.

MJ braced her hands on the ceiling and panel, to keep her in her seat, and gave him one of her "I'm not impressed" looks.

"Yeah. We've been with them for a while. They're the jokers who got us into this mess," Otto said.

"Kansas City Center, November one eight Mike Juliet. Request," MJ radioed.

"Kansas City Center. Say request," the controller replied.

"What weather are you showing on your screen?" MJ asked.

"The good news is that you're passing through the least colorful sector of the storm. The bad news is that it looks worse up ahead," the controller answered.

"Has anyone else near us reported better conditions further west?" she asked.

"Most of the traffic I'm working is up high, although there was a twin Comanche who reported a pretty good ride over near Salinas," he said.

"Good," she said. "How about a steer in that direction? We're all over the place on this line."

"Turn left, heading zero one zero. Let me know how the ride is that way," the controller said.

"Left to zero one zero, November one eight Mike Juliet," MJ reported.

"Let's see if we get any better ride on this heading," she said to Otto.

"Can't get much worse."

"Oh yes it can," MJ shot back.

The big twin dropped a quick five hundred feet and stayed there. Otto lifted the nose slightly and climbed back to eight thousand feet, adjusting the props and throttles for the climb and then back to cruise.

"How's your ride, now?" asked the controller. "My radar shows that you should be clear and on the back side of that cell you penetrated."

"Sounds right," MJ reported. "We hit a downdraft, lost five hundred feet, and then settled in. We'll stay on this heading for a while, if that's OK."

"No problem," he said. "Kansas City is pretty much surrounded with level 3s and 4s, at this time. They're not moving very fast, either. You might have a hard time getting in; we've had a number of diversions already."

"Thanks. We'll figure that out when we get there," MJ said.

"I'm going to amend your clearance to give you a better chance of getting in," he said. "Let me know when you're ready to copy.

MJ searched around the cockpit with her flashlight and found a stray pencil and piece of paper underneath her legs.

"Ready to copy," she told the controller.

"November one eight Mike Juliet, proceed direct Saint Joseph VOR, then Saint Joe one four four radial. Descend and maintain three thousand after passing Saint Joseph. Expect further clearance at zero four zero zero Zulu. Time now, zero three one five Zulu. That should keep you in the air long enough for some of the big cells to move through the area. Three thousand feet just might get you under them, too. Descend and maintain four thousand at this time," the controller instructed.

"Direct Saint Joseph, then the Saint Joseph one four four radial and three thousand. Leaving eight for four, one eight Mike Juliet," MJ read back.

"Read back is correct," said the controller. "It doesn't look too bad in front of you at the moment. Let me know if things change for the worse."

"Wilco," MJ replied.

"Bring us down slowly, Otto," MJ said. "I don't want any sudden surprises that might be lying for us down below. I'm going back and check the freight and make sure it's still snug and cozy."

"No problem, Cap," Otto said. "Down to four."

MJ walked to the back of the plane and tugged on all the straps holding the freight, then went around and checked all the fasteners that held the straps to the floor. She found one that was not secure, so she loosened the strap, reset the clamp, and pulled the strap tight. She picked up the futon and sleeping bag and brought them to the back of the plane, stowing them behind the stepladder they used to get onto the wing. After a final look around, she returned to her seat and buckled in.

"November one eight Mike Juliet, contact Kansas City approach on one three two niner five."

"One three two niner five, thanks," Otto said. He dialed in the frequency and pushed the flip-flop switch to make it active.

"Kansas City approach, November one eight Mike Juliet with you, level four thousand."

November one eight Mike Juliet, Kansas City Approach. Understand you're cleared to St. Joseph?"

"Affirm," MJ responded. "What's the weather doing?"

"It's pretty nasty. A few have gotten in, but we've had a number of diversions. Do you want to give it a try, or would you rather go to your alternate?" he asked.

"We'll give it a shot. These Dougs have a way with weather that some of the newer birds don't," she answered.

"Roger," he said "After crossing Saint Joseph, fly heading one three zero, three thousand, vectors to the final approach coarse."

"One three zero and three thousand, after Saint Joseph," MJ repeated. "One eight Mike Juliet."

251

MJ went to work setting both navigation radios to the localizer frequency and dialing up the inbound heading of 188° on the omni-bearing-selector (OBS). She set the automatic direction finder (ADF) to the locator-outer-marker frequency and put Gayly intersection in the GPS. She dialed up 1192, the minimum descent altitude, on the portable counter they kept on the console as a memory aid. She reviewed the approach plate, checked visibility requirements, reviewed the height of the obstacles near the airport, and read the missed approach procedures—there was a real probability they were going to need them. She went back to the GPS and put the Napoleon VOR in the database. They would use the GPS to get to the missed approach point during the climb-out and then set one of the navigation radios for backup, once on their way. Comfortable that everything was set, she handed the approach plates to Otto and took over flying the plane.

"We can shoot the approach with only three-eighths of a mile visibility," she said. "We ought to be able to get in."

"That'll all depend on the cells," Otto said. "If we get a break in the action, I would like it a whole lot better."

"Who wouldn't?" MJ said. "It won't be the first time we have threaded the needle, Big Guy."

"True. But that doesn't mean I have to like it," he said.

"What a wuss! Maybe you'd better let me do it, Ottoman."

"No way!" he said, tossing the approach plates back at MJ. "This one's mine. You sit over there and do the copilot thing."

"OK, Archie," she zinged back.

Otto swung his head around and glared at her.

"Sorry," she said. "I just like to see you nice and calm before challenging your flying skills."

"Thanks. Remind me to help you with a kind word or two the next time you get a good one."

"I will," she said. "I like to be puckered for the nasty ones; it gives you that edge, you know?"

"Let's just hope we won't need a change of underwear after we get down," he said. "Here's St. Joe."

Otto swung the big plane around to the new heading, reduced the power to twenty-five inches, and began the descent.

"November one eight Mike Juliet, Approach. Can you proceed direct Gayly intersection?" the controller asked.

"Affirmative," MJ reported.

"Roger. Proceed direct Gayly. Cleared for the ILS one-nine left approach. Contact tower on one two eight point two. Good luck."

"What's going on with the weather on the field?" MJ asked.

"I'm showing a level three, maybe four, over the field, moving southwesterly."

"Thanks. Might be talking with you real soon," she said. "See ya."

MJ dialed in the tower frequency and keyed her mic.

"Kansas City tower, November one eight Mike Juliet, inbound to Gayly."

"November one eight Mike Juliet, cleared to land runway one-nine-left. Winds variable, two zero zero to two five zero, one five knots, gusting to two five. Caution, wind shear," the tower controller reported.

"Cleared to land, one-nine left," MJ reported. "This ought to be interesting, Otto. Give me your best shot."

"Get the before landing stuff, MJ."

MJ reached up and switched on the electric boost pumps. She tested the brakes with her feet and watched the

255

drop and return of system hydraulic
pressure. The plane began to jump
and roll with turbulence.

"Here's Gayly," MJ called out.
"Lexey next."

Otto had already begun turning the
plane toward the airport when
the localizer's course deviation
indicator began to move. He reduced
the power to twenty inches.

"Flaps one-quarter," he said.

"Flaps one," MJ responded.

Otto saw the glide slope come
alive and drift downward as they
approached the outer marker. When it
was just above the horizon line, he
called for gear down.

"Gear coming down," MJ confirmed.

Otto trimmed the nose up and
slowed the plane to one hundred
knots. Turbulence was bouncing and
shaking them to the point where it
was difficult for Otto to keep his
feet on the rudder pedals. He
wrestled with the column trying to
keep the wings level and the
airspeed constant.

"Keep your speed up, Otto, and be ready to kick in some power if the wind shears on us."

Otto tried to answer, but a jolt from turbulence almost cost him a piece of his tongue. He decided to keep quiet and fly the plane.

Otto pushed the prop levers forward just as the airspeed dropped from one hundred to eighty knots. He moved the throttles forward to twenty-five inches and watched the airspeed indicator and vertical speed indicator. The airspeed indicator began to rise and the vertical speed indicator jumped to a one thousand feet-per-minute indicated climb rate. He reduced the manifold pressure by three inches.

"We've got over ten-thousand feet of runway, Otto. Bring her in hot if you have to," MJ offered.

"Let me know as soon as you have anything," Otto ordered.

"Gear is down and locked, pumps on, flaps are one-quarter," she reported.

257

He continued to wrestle with the big plane, trying to keep the CDI and glide slope needles as close together as possible. He glanced at the altimeter; it read 1850 feet, then 1750.

"I've got lights, continue," MJ called out. "Looking good. Come right a bit."

"Minimums," MJ reported.

Otto looked up and saw the runway lights in front of him; he was just left of the centerline, crabbing into the wind. He pulled the throttles back and dipped the right wing into the wind, counteracting with a lot of left rudder to keep the nose of the big bird aligned with the centerline. He held the Gooney Bird off the ground as long as he could, bleeding off the excess airspeed. The big DC-3 settled onto the runway, and Otto pushed the control wheel forward to keep her there. He pulled the left throttle to the stop but left some power on the right engine to counter the weathervane effect the crosswind was creating. He danced on the rudder pedals and put the right aileron all the way into the wind. The plane slowed to 60 knots; Otto pulled gently on the control-wheel column until the tail wheel settled onto the runway.

"After stuff," he said to MJ.

MJ turned off the boost pumps and opened the cowl flaps. She turned off the landing lights as soon as they turned off the runway.

"Nice job," the tower controller said. "We showed a wind gust of thirty-five knots just before you touched down. Contact ground, point-niner."

"Thanks," Otto said. "Ground point-nine."

They taxied the Gooney to the general aviation ramp and shut it down. The last leg had eaten up their duty time, so they would not be able to continue for another ten hours.

"I'm sorry those folks in Chicago are going to have to wait a little longer for their freight," Otto

Rick Byam

said. But I'll tell you, after that experience, I don't think I want to go anywhere *but* bed."

"Ya done good," MJ poked at him, as she shined her flashlight on her face, crossed her eyes, and stuck out her tongue.

"Cute, real cute. And you call yourself an adult?" asked Otto.

"No, I call myself MJ," she laughed. "That *was* a tough one, Otto. I'm glad to see you've been paying attention all these years. Let's lock her up and find some place to crash. Pun intended."

NINETEEN

"November one eight Mike Juliet understands cleared to Midway via Lakes Four Departure, Peatun, direct. Climb and maintain niner thousand, departure on one thirty-two ninety-five, six two three eight in the box," Otto said, reading back the clearance.

"Read-back is correct. Contact ground point eight for taxi. Have a nice flight," the controller said.

"Looks like we might finally see Chicago, MJ," Otto said.

"Maybe. We still have six-and-a-half hours of flight time to deal with, Ottoman. Do you need to go potty before we head out?"

"I'm good."

"Didn't we get topped off last night?" she asked him.

"Yeah, why?"

"Did you pay for it, yet?" she asked.

"Of course. What's with the twenty questions?"

"It looks like the fuel truck is coming this way. Somebody must have gotten his signals crossed," she said.

The fuel truck from the FBO pulled around to the back of the left wing, facing the cargo door. Otto and MJ heard the driver honk the horn twice.

"Go back there and see what they want, Otto. Tell them we don't need fuel."

"OK, Cap."

Otto climbed out of the right seat and made his way back to the cargo doors. He unlatched the right side, swung the door open, and found himself staring into the barrel of a nine-millimeter handgun.

"Wha. . . ?" he stammered.

"Shut up. Don't make a sound," the man who was holding the gun said. "Pass down that ladder."

The door opened further, and Otto saw a second man pointing a gun at his head. The first man grabbed the short ladder and hooked it into the slots on the floor of the DC-3. Still pointing the gun at Otto, he climbed inside.

Both men were dressed in overalls with the insignia of the FBO over the left pocket and wore baseball caps. They had black hair, dark skin, and deep dark eyes. One of them had a ponytail, but the other had his hair neatly trimmed above the ears. They spoke with Spanish accents.

"What are you doing?" Otto questioned.

"We're going to borrow your plane, Amigo," he said.

The second man returned to the truck and came back with a third man walking in front of him. They both climbed into the airplane and walked up to the cabin, where MJ sat looking at the intruders with disbelief.

"What are you doing in my airplane?" she demanded. "What do you want?"

"We want you to take us for a little ride, Pretty Lady," the man with the ponytail said. "It's a nice day for a plane ride, don't you think?"

"Get out of here, now!" she said, as she started out of her seat and toward him.

The man swung the pistol and caught MJ on the forehead, stunning her; a trickle of blood ran down her face. She sank back into her seat, holding her head with her right hand.

"You son-of-a-bitch," Otto said, and lunged for the man in front of him.

The second of the two men caught him from behind with the butt of the pistol, dropping him to the deck.

"YOU BASTARDS!" MJ screamed and went after the man, again.

He swung the pistol but this time MJ held her arms up to block the blow. She grabbed him by the throat with her left hand and grabbed his ponytail with her right. He smashed his fist into her stomach, and she fell back into her seat fighting for breath.

"You're a feisty bitch, but not too smart, Muchacha," he said, coughing from the attack on his throat. "Any more of that, and I will put a bullet right between those pretty blue eyes of yours."

"Up yours!" she said, grunting the words with what breath she could muster.

The man raised the pistol to strike her again.

"Wait, Gussman!" interrupted the third man. "You need her to fly. Beating her senseless won't get you what you want. And if you kill her, who's going to fly you to Chicago?" he asked.

MJ looked in the direction of the man who just spoke. She knew that voice.

"Ned? Ned Greenlawn?" she asked.

"Hello, MJ."

"What the hell's going on?" she asked.

"It's a long story, MJ. They're drug dealers. You'd better do what they want; these guys don't fool around."

"Drug dealers!" she yelled. "What the hell are you doing with drug dealers?"

"I'm a hostage. Do you remember the first village we flew to when you first came to Mexico to fly with me?" he asked.

"Yes, of course," she answered.

"Well, they are being held by these guys, too, just to make sure this trip goes without a hitch."

"The whole village?" she asked.

"The whole village," he answered. "They are going to kill them all if we don't make this trip."

"Ned, I haven't seen you in over ten years. How the hell did you get me involved in this?"

"They didn't want to attract attention, so they wanted me to find them a small operator. You're the only one I knew who was an independent and somewhat incognito," Ned answered. "You wouldn't be surrounded by a lot of other company aircraft on your stops. It would be easier to get to you."

"But how did you get involved with them in the first place?" she asked.

267

"Bad luck, I guess. They used me to haul drugs out of South America into Mexico. I didn't know it at the time. They had packaged the stuff to look like medical waste, so I never gave it a second thought. Who would have thought that drug dealers would have taken advantage of a medical outreach program to distribute their illegal drugs? I sure didn't."

"That still doesn't explain why you're doing this," she said.

"During one of the pick-ups in Peru, I dropped a package labeled "medical waste." The wrapping broke on one end, and there was white powder leaking out. I knew right away what it was. I was really pissed. I called the authorities to report it; they came and took the entire load away. Shortly after they left, another group of men showed up. They told me I made a mistake calling the police, and then introduced me to the chief, who was standing there with them. They told me that if I wanted to continue working with the missionary groups throughout the region and keep them protected, I was going to have to do penance. I asked them what they meant, but they just told me they would be in touch when the time came."

"So this is your penance?" she asked.

"I'm afraid so, MJ. They were waiting for me in Tepotzlan. They told me they needed a favor. They had a shipment that they needed to get to Chicago from Mexico and they wanted me to find a way to do it, quietly and quickly. I told them I wouldn't do it, so they killed Antonio to make their point. They told me that they would kill my whole family if I didn't do what they wanted. I made the mistake of telling them that I didn't have any family; that's when they decided to hold the village hostage. They knew about the village near Oaxaca from their sources working with the guerillas in the area. They just called the commandant and told him to surround the village until further notice. I can't let them kill all those people, MJ. I don't think I ever told you, but that's the village Mariana came from."

"No, you didn't. So I'm it? You're making me the savior?"

"You're the only one I know up here in the States, MJ. I'm sorry; I really am. We do this trip, and it's over. You go back to flying the friendly skies, and I'll go back to my jungles," he said.

"I still don't understand why you need me?" she said. "Couldn't they just buy . . . or steal . . . a plane and have you drive it?"

"No. First of all, that would raise too many flags. It would look too suspicious, especially after 9/11. A new registry flying from the Mexican border inland to Chicago? They would be watching it like a hawk. Someone like you, who is already making these trips all over the country, would draw less attention," he said. "The other factor is that I don't know how to operate in this environment very well. Remember that most of my flying is out of contact with any aviation authority. I'd be lost if I had to do this by myself. I don't think it would take the FAA very long to figure out there was an amateur hauling freight from the Mexican border to points north."

"How did you know I would be landing in Kansas City?" she asked.

"An educated guess?"

"No, really, Ned. How did you know?" she asked, again.

"It was the most logical choice for a fuel stop between Phoenix and Chicago, MJ, especially running at night. The confirmation came from your copilot," he said.

"Otto?"

"Otto," he said. "The drivers in Phoenix asked him where you were headed, and he told them. You might want to tell him to keep his cards a little closer to his chest, especially in this new age of terrorism we live in."

"How did they get their stuff to look like it was from the auto plants? How did you get on this field? Security is a bear," she said.

271

"They have friends in high places, MJ. You can't imagine what you can buy if you have the money."

"Great!" she said. "So what now?" she asked.

"You and I will take this stuff to Chicago. That's all," he said.

"That's all?" she asked. "Do you think I'm going to let myself be hijacked with a load of drugs and just forget it?"

"Not exactly," Ned said. "They're going to keep Otto, just to make sure you do your part."

At that moment, Otto was coming around, and the man that hit him grabbed him by the back of the shirt and hauled him to his feet.

"C'mon, Hero," he said. "We're going for a little ride. Greenlawn, give me those coveralls!" he ordered.

Ned removed his coveralls and the man made Otto put them on. The two men put Otto between them and dragged him to the door. He looked back at Ned and MJ.

"Are you OK, MJ?" he asked.

"Yeah, I'm OK, Otto. At least for now," she said. "Don't do anything crazy, Ottoman. I'll see you as soon as this is over."

"How did it ever get started, MJ?" he asked.

"It's a bad dream, Otto," she said. "Go sleep it off; I'll catch up with you later."

Otto appeared dazed and stared back with a confused look on his face. The man with the ponytail put the gun in his pocket and climbed down the ladder. Otto went next; the other man followed. They kept Otto between them until they got to the fuel truck and then forced him inside.

"He'll be all right, MJ," Ned assured her. "These guys just want to make sure this load gets where it needs to be. I guess they've gone through a lot of trouble on this one."

MJ looked back into the cargo area as the man with the ponytail climbed back inside. He pulled up the ladder and closed the cargo doors.

"Where's he going?" she asked.

"Miguel's coming with us," Ned answered. "He wants to make sure we don't make any unnecessary calls on the radio or land where we're not supposed to."

"Seems like overkill, doesn't it, Ned?" she asked. "They've got a whole village of hostages and Otto. Do they really think we would do something stupid and allow them to kill all those people and Otto, too?"

"They are, obviously, taking no chances," he answered. "Let's hope that nothing goes wrong."

TWENTY

"November one eight Mike Juliet, Chicago Center," the controller said.

"Chicago Center, one eight Mike Juliet," MJ answered.

"After crossing Capital, descend and maintain five thousand, proceed direct Midway."

"After Capital, down to five, direct Midway, one eight Mike Juliet."

"Almost home," Ned said.

275

"None too soon for me," MJ responded. "How am I going to get in touch with Otto?"

"Once the freight is picked up, they'll give you a number where you can reach him," Ned answered. "After that, you'll just have to figure out how to team up again."

"Greenlawn, I need your help back here," Miguel called out.

"What does he want?" MJ asked Ned.

"I, um, don't know. Let me go back and check. You OK up here?" he asked.

"Yeah, I'm fine. We still have a ways to go, although this routing will get us there a little sooner."

"Let me go see what he wants; I'll be back."

Ned went back to the cargo area and closed the cockpit door behind him. MJ stared at the transponder for a long time before she gave up on the idea of selecting 7500, the code for a hijacking. She thought about Otto; she thought about what she was hauling and what she was doing; she thought about her business; and she thought about how she could lose everything by not reporting this to the Feds. Right now, she just wanted to get this over with and get Otto out of their hands.

"November one eight Mike Juliet, contact Chicago Approach Control on one one niner point three five."

"One nineteen thirty-five," MJ responded. She dialed in the new frequency and checked in with Chicago Approach.

Ned had been gone a long time, and MJ was getting curious. She trimmed the plane for level flight, got up, and slowly opened the cockpit door a crack. She saw the two men assembling metal casks together; they were combining one piece from the load they picked up in Phoenix with a piece from the crates that were put on in El Paso. Ned held one piece on top of the other while Miguel bolted them together. Once joined, they put them back onto the pallet and tied them down.

"What the hell are you doing?" she yelled at Ned, surprised to see him working with Miguel.

Miguel drew his pistol and pointed it at MJ. Ned held his hand up in front of Miguel.

"Don't! I'll take care of this," he said.

Ned walked up to MJ, took her by the arm, and led her back into the cockpit.

"Sit down, MJ!" he said. "Fly the plane!"

"What are you doing back there?" she asked again, the fear rising in her gut.

"I'm afraid that I've been less than honest with you, MJ," he said, as he sat down in the right seat and put on his headset.

"Those aren't drugs, are they?" she asked.

"No. There are no drugs on the plane," he answered.

278

"Then, what are we doing? What are those things you two are putting together?" she asked.

"Those are a special concoction I came up with to solve a little problem we've been having," he said. "My years with the Green Beanies were not in vain, you see. They taught me to be innovative."

"What *are* you talking about?" she said.

"The top half of those canisters is filled with sodium cyanide, MJ," he said. "The bottom contains citric acid. There is an impermeable membrane between the two so that the chemicals won't mix . . . unless, of course, there is sufficient impact to break the membrane and marry the two chemicals. Now that's an ugly wedding, MJ; one you wouldn't want to be anywhere near."

She couldn't believe what she was hearing. "Cyanide gas! Why would you want to make cyanide gas?"

"You remember your basic chemistry, I see. We have a little

279

business to take care of in Chicago; however, we have to be careful how we go about it."

MJ noticed that Ned was now talking about "we" and "I", when referring to this project. His demeanor had also changed. He was no longer the friendly flyer she once knew; his tone had turned sinister.

"Ned, what are you talking about? What are you going to do with those things?"

"We are going to assist America's drug czar and take out one of the biggest drug bosses in the US," he answered. "But, you see, he's not an easy target. For one thing, he moves around a lot, like Saddam Hussein. He stays in the same basic neighborhood, but we never know in which house or building he's going to be. It makes an ambush a little difficult to plan and execute. Excuse the pun, please. So, since we are in the midst of a war on drugs, I thought a little bombing would be in order. That way, we just have to get close; we don't actually have to hit him."

"What are you saying? Are you telling me that you're going to gas an entire neighborhood, just to get this one guy?"

"Precisely!"

"Ned, that's murder! Think of all the innocent people that will be killed."

"There's collateral damage in any war, MJ," he said. Besides, we're *all* innocent! Aren't we? It's just circumstance that takes away that innocence. I imagine there are quite a few in that neighborhood who have lost that innocence by their own choice. Maybe if they didn't have a drug habit, they would have gotten a better education, a better job, and a better life for themselves. Or maybe it's the other way around. No matter. They're already dying a slow death; I'm just going to speed things up for them a bit."

"This is *crazy*," she said.

"Actually, it's quite ingenious, if I do say so myself. al-Qaeda has opened up a whole new way of doing business since September 11, 2001.

281

In fact, it's important that everyone thinks that they are the responsible party for this heinous crime we are about to commit."

"Why?"

"As I said, this guy is one of the biggest bosses in the country. If his people find out it was the Colombian Cartel that took out their boss and his neighborhood, the drug trade is going to take on a whole new face. You would never see another ounce of coke allowed in from the cartel; they would dry up and blow away with no market for their product. I'd be out of business."

"*You* would be out of business?" she asked. "What *happened* to you, Ned?"

"Ten years is a long time, MJ," he said. "A lot can happen."

"I'm sorry, but it's a bit of a stretch for me to connect missionary work with drug trafficking."

"Not so much. The only difference is money. The rest is the same:

bringing supplies and relief to those in need. It's just a different kind of need; that's all. God wears a different face for different people."

"When did this start for you?" she asked. "Not while I was with you, I hope."

"No, MJ," he said. "Actually, that was the best year of my life. You were great, and we had a lot of fun, didn't we? It was a few years down the road. Finding good help who will work for food and shelter is a tough row to hoe. The quality of the flyers I had to work with steadily decreased until it seemed I was doing everything myself; the yo-yo in the other seat was just for show. After a couple of months on the job, they were either drunk or stoned most of the time. I kept them on as long as I could, or at least until I could find a fresh body to stick in the right seat. It got downright discouraging."

"I can understand your frustration, Ned, but I don't see the drug connection."

"The story I told you earlier, about discovering drugs among the medical waste, wasn't exactly accurate," he said.

"Nothing about this trip is exactly accurate," she replied.

"Yeah. I guess you're right about that. Anyway, I was getting tired, MJ, and I had to start thinking about my retirement. It scared the shit out of me when I did, though. I could add up what I had going for me on one hand. That plane certainly wasn't an asset; it ate up funds as fast as I could secure them. I looked down the road and I didn't see a damn thing."

"What about your time with the Army?" she asked. "Wasn't there anything for you if you retired?"

"I wasn't in long enough. I had some of the GI Bill left, but not enough to get me any real education that would help my cause. I had been so busy all those years flying around down there, I never had time to stop and look forward for more than a week at a time. When I did, I panicked."

"So then what?" she asked. "You just checked into the local drug warehouse and offered your services?"

"Something like that," he laughed. "You've got to remember that I've been flying around Central and South America, as well as Mexico, for quite some time. And the jungle has eyes, as the saying goes. These guys aren't stupid. They saw me as a regular fixture in the aviation infrastructure, tooling around from here to there without any hassles from any authority figures. To them, it was a free pass to a new distribution network. To me, it became a retirement plan, kind of like a 401K, except they were putting all the bucks in the bank; I didn't have to contribute anything but my time. They pay very well, MJ. Did I tell you that?"

"No, I can't say that you did. I can't believe you sold out, Ned. After all those years helping people. Everything you saw in Vietnam: the pain, the suffering, the guys hooked on drugs who died a slow death once they returned to the

States. I thought you had higher ideals that that."

"So did I, until I realized that no one was going to help me. You know, when you give and give and give, for what seems to be your entire life, and then you turn around with your hand out and no one's there, it's scary, MJ. I saw myself as some burned-out bush pilot without a pot to piss in, hanging around street corners looking for a handout. Or worse, some derelict expatriated American roaming the streets of some Latin American city by day, getting drunk by night, and sleeping under a piece of cardboard in a park somewhere. It wasn't a pretty picture I was seeing, MJ."

"That was *your* picture, Ned. You could have painted a better one if you wanted to."

"Well, that's what I did. I painted myself into a castle, with swimming pools, marble floors, Roman columns, statues; you know, the celebrity package. I liked that painting a whole lot better than the one I was facing."

"So how did you get involved with the shipments?"

"Part of what I told you was true. Some of these guys were slipping a few packages in with the medical waste and supplies, and I found out about it; so I made them a deal. I agreed to carry more of their product with my regular supplies if they would help me build a 'retirement fund,' so to speak. I had them open a bank account in my name and put a little something in it every time I made a shipment. They're business people, MJ, and they saw the advantage of my offer. I built up a pretty good stash."

"OK, fine. But what's *this* all about? This isn't about hauling drugs; this is *murder*."

"Is it? We allow thousands of kids to starve every year. More people die on the highways each year than were killed in Vietnam over its entire twenty-year history. We poison our water, our air, and our food. We bomb civilians during our righteous campaigns around the world, and we support governments that kill thousands of their own

287

people, usually with weapons that we supplied. Do we call *that* murder, MJ?"

"It's not the same, Ned, no matter what spin you put on it. *This* is premeditated murder, and a lot of people who are trying to make a good life for themselves and their families are going to die for no reason. You can't *do* this, Ned," she pleaded.

"I don't have a choice, MJ. It's him or me. If I don't help the cartel get this guy, they're going to take everything I've saved. There won't be anything left to show for the last five years of taking all that risk."

"Do you *really* think they're going to just let you walk away, especially after what you told me about not connecting this, this . . . assassination to the cartel?"

"Yes, I do. I put together a tight plan that will leave no trail leading back to the cartel. Everyone is going to see this as another terrorist act, perpetrated by al-

Qaeda or some other extremist group."

"Aren't you forgetting something, Ned?" she asked.

"Like what?"

"If we stray from this route, this flight plan, for more than a couple of minutes, we're going to have F-16s all over us, like hornets on an apple," she said.

"I love your little country analogies, MJ. I always did," he said. "Yes, you're right. Once we execute this plan, we're going to have very little time to pull it off. Fortunately, the target is just slightly off our route, especially now that they've given us direct. I thought I was going to have to cancel IFR and continue VFR, but they've made it easy for me. I figure we'll have enough time to drop low over the rooftops, make one good-sized circle, drop enough of the canisters to ensure success, and get to our escape point before the F-16s can get off the ground and get anywhere near us."

"We're in a *plane*, Ned, and they have very sophisticated equipment aboard those things. They aren't going to have any trouble finding us."

"As soon as we make the drops, we will head due west. Just outside of the suburbs, we've put together an ingenious little movie set. It shouldn't take more than five minutes to get there. We land the plane and get picked up by others in this operation. We'll be changing cars five different times. By the time someone comes snooping around asking the neighbors what they know, they won't have a clue as to what happened to us. This little movie set, as I like to call it, has been seeded with all kinds of links leading to Al-Qaeda, including hair and saliva that will provide investigators with DNA samples linked to known members of the group. There will be Al-Qaeda propaganda, videos from Osama, instructions on how to make these cyanide gas bombs, everything. The Chicago bosses will think they were victims of circumstance, not revenge."

"So what's this *revenge* for?" she asked.

"There was a change of leadership in Chicago about a month ago. It came about when the Don passed away, from old age no less, and his son took command. We had been working with the son for many years, and everything seemed copacetic. What we didn't know was that he was just following orders from his father until the old guy passed away. Meanwhile, he was setting up new deals with a Mexican cartel from the South and Turks from the East. He was going to flood the country with cheap product from his new partners, dry up the Colombian connection, and then raise prices, virtually doubling the profits. His father believed in loyalty and treating business partners fairly, but his son, great American businessman that he is, only has eyes for the bottom line. As you can see, this is bad business for my compadres. They are betting another change in Chicago might bring a more reasonable business partner to the negotiating table."

"Unbelievable," she said. "And what about me?"

"You'll be coming with us. I convinced them that I could keep you quiet in exchange for your life . . . and Otto's, too. We'll fix it so it looks like you were both kidnapped, tied, gagged, and left in separate abandoned warehouses, and that al-Qaeda members stole your plane to do their dirty work. You'll get your plane back, eventually, and you two can go back to flying America's friendly skies. Pretty good, eh?"

"It sucks, Ned. That's the dumbest thing I've ever heard. Do you really think that I can go through the rest of my life like nothing happened after I watch you and that other asshole back there drop poisonous gas onto a major metropolitan area?"

"Careful, MJ. I *can* fly this plane by myself; you know that. I cut this deal with them because I like you. I wasn't kidding when I said that was the best year of *my* life: flying with you, enjoying your enthusiasm for aviation, and seeing your lust for life. Don't make me be the one to end it. Please. Just do as you're told, and you and Otto can walk away from this."

"You're a sick man, Ned Greenlawn," MJ spit back.

"November one eight Mike Juliet, squawk 7700, turn left heading two eight five. Follow the F-16 coming up on your left side. Acknowledge."

"Wha . . .?" Ned stammered in amazement. "What are they doing? Why are they intercepting? Don't answer that call, MJ!"

Ned switched the radio frequency, so that MJ couldn't respond to the controller's request, and pushed the nose of the Gooney bird steeply toward the ground.

"WHAT ARE YOU DOING!" MJ screamed at him. "Ned, you can't outrun an F-16!"

"Maybe not, but I can make it difficult for him to shoot us down."

An F-16 screamed past the left side of the airplane, banked hard right, and pulled up and around the DC-3.

"YOU ARE GONNA GET US KILLED, NED!" MJ screamed at him, again.

"Not before I finish what I came to do," he said.

"It's over, Ned. There's not going to be any killing. It won't do you any good; you won't be able to collect any of that money."

"You're right, MJ. . . as usual. But I still think it was a great plan; we'll just have to modify it a bit."

The DC-3 fell from the sky until it looked like it was going to collide with the rooftops below. At the last possible instant, Ned pulled on the control column and leveled her. There was a crash from the cargo compartment, and MJ feared the worse: that a canister had slammed into the fuselage and they would soon all be gassed. She looked back through the cabin door and saw Miguel lying on the floor next to one of the pallets, blood streaming from his right temple. She figured the negative Gs caught him by surprise and floated him like an astronaut-in-training, and when Ned pulled out of the dive, gravity slammed him into the pallet. Ned turned to see what she was looking at and saw Miguel unconscious and bleeding on the cargo floor.

"Shit!"

"C'mon, Ned. End it!" MJ ordered. "Let me talk to these guys before they blow us out of the sky," she pleaded.

Ned unbuckled his seatbelt and drew a gun from under his shirt. He pointed it at MJ as he got up and started toward the rear.

"I'm real sorry about this, MJ," he said. "But if you don't keep this plane on an even keel for me for the next few minutes, I'm going to be forced to blow your brains out."

"I can't let you do this, Ned. You don't have to do it, either. The plan's a bust, Ned. Give it up!"

Ned drew back the hammer of the pistol with his thumb and continued to point it at MJ.

"Don't make me do it, MJ. Just a couple of minutes, that's all I'm asking."

MJ looked into his eyes and saw pain and fear. She turned in her seat and faced forward, trimming the plane slightly. Ned turned and started for the cargo area. As soon as he was out of the cockpit, she grabbed the control column, pulled back as hard as she could, slammed the prop and throttles levers forward, jumped on the left rudder, and turned the control wheel hard left. The Gooney bird rolled quickly over on its left wing and then onto its back. MJ released a little pressure on the control column and continued the roll, praying the big bird would hold together. She let the plane dive closer to the ground before she brought the wings level and lifted the nose to level flight. She unbuckled her seatbelt, jumped out of her seat, and ran to the back of the plane. Ned was on the floor holding his head in his hands and groaning; his gun was lying nearby. MJ grabbed the pistol, stuck it into her belt, and secured some rope from the back. She tied Ned quickly, using a calf roping technique she had learned as a young girl in Montana. She was running back toward the cockpit when the plane suddenly shuddered and there was a loud noise from underneath her feet. Through the side widows she saw an F-16 fly from underneath the plane, round out, and begin another pass at the Gooney. She strapped herself in, flipped the transponder to 7500, and dialed 121.5 into the #1 radio.

"DON'T SHOOT! JESUS CHRIST, DO NOT SHOOT! THIS PLANE IS FULL OF CHEMICALS! DON'T SHOOT!" she screamed into her microphone.

She watched as the F-16 completed its course reversal and leveled itself at the DC-3.

"DO YOU HEAR ME? DON'T SHOOT, GODDAMMIT. THE PLANE'S FULL OF HAZARDOUS MATERIALS!"

The F-16 headed directly at her, but she didn't dare take any evasive action for fear they would construe it to be an aggressive or non-compliant maneuver. The Falcon screamed over the top of the Gooney bird so close that MJ thought it was going to hit her. The vortices from the fast flying jet rocked the DC-3, and MJ had to fight for control.

"November one eight Mike Juliet, the DC-3 just south of Midway Field. This is Lightning Strike Leader at your six-o'clock. Do you copy?" the voice on the radio said.

"I HEAR YOU! I HEAR YOU! DO NOT SHOOT! THIS PLANE IS FULL OF HAZMAT! IF WE GO DOWN, A LOT OF PEOPLE ARE GOING TO DIE! DO YOU HEAR *ME*?" she yelled into the microphone.

"Roger, understand your cargo is dangerous. Are you Carlson?" he asked.

"Affirmative," she answered.

"Say status," the voice commanded.

"I have about one point five hours of fuel; there are three on board: one is dead, I think, and the other is subdued," she answered.

An F-16 appeared off her left wing and slightly forward; it had its landing gear and flaps extended so that it could fly alongside the slow moving Doug. Another F-16 appeared on the right side of the plane, apparently inspecting the situation.

"What about the chemicals?" the pilot asked.

"It's some sort of device that is rigged to mix on impact to create cyanide gas. It's all tied down. It should be OK if I can land this plane normally," she answered.

"Roger. I want you to follow me. We're going to take you to a remote field not too far east of here. Do not deviate in any way from the course heading. Do you understand?" he asked.

"Completely," she answered.

"Leader, we have a problem," another voice cut in. She's leaking fluids from the undercarriage," he said.

MJ looked at the hydraulic pressure gauges; the pressure was dropping steadily.

"Carlson, check your fuel status," ordered the first voice.

MJ switched the fuel selector valves to check the status of each tank; the news wasn't good.

"I'm showing minimum fuel," she said. "The hydraulic fluid levels are dropping off, too."
"We probably punctured the lines when we fired on you," the first voice said. "Stand by."

MJ put the fuel selector valves on the fullest tanks and checked the gauges.

"One eight Mike Juliet, change of plans. Do you believe the containers are stable in their current condition?" the pilot asked.

"Affirmative," she answered. "They said it would take impact to mix the two chemicals and make the cyanide gas. Everything is tied down."

"Roger. Your fuel status doesn't give us much of an option. You are lined up for a straight-in approach to runway four-left at Midway. They are foaming the runway, as we speak. Equipment will be standing by for your arrival."

300

"Understand four-left at Midway. I need to leave the radio for a minute. I have a can of hydraulic fluid in the back that I can dump into the system at the last moment. That way, I'll have flaps, brakes, and gear for the landing," she told the F-16 pilot along side.

"Report back up," he said.

"Wilco," she said.

MJ climbed out of her seat, ran back to the tail-end storage area, and grabbed a can of hydraulic fluid. Ned was conscious, but said nothing as she passed by. She stopped long enough to check the security of the ropes, but showed no sympathy for his condition.

"Back with you," she reported to her escorts.

"Roger," he replied. "You are eight miles from touchdown."

The Gooney Bird's right engine began to sputter. The fuel gauge indicated empty. She turned on the boost pump, pushed the mixture lever

301

into emergency rich, and switched to the other tank. The engine came to life for another couple of minutes and then quit. She quickly feathered and secured it.

"Number two is gone," she reported.

"You are five miles from touchdown," her escort advised her.

MJ had the runway in site and was lining up with the centerline when the number one engine began to cough and sputter. She turned on the boost pump and threw the mixture lever into emergency rich, as before.

"C'mon big girl. We've been here before; you can do this. We've gone through too much to give up now. C'mon! C'mon!" she pleaded.

She could see that the plane was sinking below the glide path by the two red lights on the VASI, the vertical approach slope indicator. She eased the throttle for the left engine forward. She checked the trim on the plane and then jumped up to pour hydraulic fluid into the system. She wasn't concerned about the flaps, but it would be nice to be able to extend the gear and have some brakes on the rollout. The number one engine sputtered again. MJ jumped back into her seat and pumped the throttle a couple of times.

"C'mon, dammit! Just a little further," she coaxed.

"Three miles from touchdown," the F-16 pilot announced.

The number one engine gave a final cough, backfired, and quit. MJ punched the feathering button and secured the engine. After she made sure that the mags and master were off and the mixtures were full aft, she turned the fuel valves to off.

"Number one is gone," she said.

"You can make it; you can make it," the F-16 pilot said, urging her on.

"Too heavy," she said. "I don't think I can glide that far."

"You can do it, Carlson," he said. "Stay with it!"

303

MJ trimmed the bird for best glide, 95 to 105 knots, and kept it clean, no flaps. When she thought she was going to make the runway, she reached for the gear handle and tried to lower the gear. There was still some pressure in the system, but nothing was registering on the gear-down pressure gauge.

"Did the gear extend?" she asked the F-16 driver on her left wing.

"Negative," he said.

"You must have got the lines, or something," she said.

While MJ was distracted with the gear, the plane lost valuable altitude. The runway was no longer an option.

"I'm not going to make the runway," she said. I'm going to be short. Let's hope I can keep it soft, gentlemen," she said.

"Understood," her escort said. "Good luck, Carlson."

"Thanks. Let's hope I don't need it."

The two F-16s followed along most of the way down, then turned away from her, retracted their landing gear, and climbed away from the airport.

MJ thought about the cargo weight and its distribution. She did a quick calculation to determine just how slowly she could fly the plane and still maintain control—around 55 to 60 knots with flaps down, she thought. She glanced at the hydraulic pressure gauge and figured she had some pressure available, so she pushed the flap lever all the way down and left it there. She could feel the plane struggle against the drag, as she monitored the airspeed indicator. She looked left and right of the runway, hoping she might see a better option for putting the plane down off the field, but decided straight ahead was her best bet. She had the plane going as slowly as she possibly could, as the approach lights and fixtures began to pass under the fuselage of the plane. When she heard them begin to scrape on the

305

aluminum of the plane's belly, she pulled back on the control column and held the nose up as long as she could. The plane stalled quickly and settled into the lighting fixtures below her. The plane creaked and groaned as it slid along the soft, sandy soil, while the metal of the approach light system drummed out a tune on the fuselage. MJ tried to keep the plane going straight by using the rudder pedals, but the thrashing the plane was taking from all the obstacles it was plowing through quickly made it a useless gesture. MJ braced herself against the side of her seat by pushing against the panel in front of her and the one overhead. The noise of the crash reached a crescendo and then came to a sudden halt.

MJ sat motionless for a moment and then remembered her cargo. If any of the containers had ruptured, she figured she would only have a couple of minutes before the gas reached her. Quickly, she unlatched the overhead escape hatch, pushed the panel out of the way, and climbed out to the top of the plane. She felt something pinch her mid-section and lifted her shirt to see what it was. Ned's gun. "Don't need them to find this on me," she thought. She removed it from her waistband and dropped it back into the plane.

There were vehicles coming from everywhere: fire engines, a Hazmat team, police cars, FAA vehicles, military jeeps and trucks. She started to walk toward the tail of the plane when a black van pulled up, and a SWAT team jumped out and told her not to move. They were wearing gas masks and pointing M-16 rifles at her.

"Get me away from this plane," she said to them. "I don't know if the canisters have ruptured or not."

"All right," the one in front said. "Move slowly; keep your hands where we can see them."

MJ kept her hands out to her side for balance and continued walking to the tail of the plane. She slid down onto the horizontal stabilizer and jumped to the ground. Two members of the SWAT team seized her immediately. She was cuffed and rushed to the unit's van.

TWENTY-ONE

"That was a nice piece of flying, Carlson," the tall, thin pilot said, standing just inside the doorway of the conference room.

MJ took another sip of her coffee and rested it on the table. She kept both hands wrapped around the paper cup and stared into the center of the black liquid.

"Are you the jet-jock that filled my plane full of holes?" she asked, not looking up at the man who spoke to her.

"I'm afraid so, Ms. Carlson," he said.

"It's MJ," she said, looking up at him.

"Excuse me, Ma'am?"

"Everyone calls me MJ, Captain Stewart," she repeated, taking his name and rank from the flight suit he was wearing.

"It's Mike," he came back. "I'm sure you understand, MJ, that we really didn't have much choice in the matter. You did not follow our orders or answer our calls; there *is* no intermediate phase, especially after September 11th. We shoot to remove the threat and protect lives."

MJ lifted the coffee to her lips and took a long drink. She put the cup down and looked at Mike.

"Only in this case, Mike, you could have been responsible for the deaths of thousands of people if that plane crashed."

"Ms. Carlson, Captain Stewart was following orders—very *specific* orders," Colonel Ferguson cut in.

"You may want to re-evaluate your battle plans, Colonel," MJ said. "That wasn't a jumbo jet full of jet fuel over southern Chicago. It was a DC-3 that had burned off over six-and-a-half hours of fuel, proceeding according to its flight plan, at least up until the time Ned grabbed the controls."

"My point exactly," Colonel Ferguson said. "We were left with no choice."

"There are always choices, Colonel," MJ retorted.

"All right, all of you. That's enough!" said Gregg Hanscom, Senior Field Agent, Central District, Federal Bureau of Investigation. "We can't change what took place three days ago; we can only be thankful that Ms. Carlson was able to gain control of her flight and land the airplane, averting a major catastrophe in the process. I think that we all owe her a great deal of gratitude."

"As I said, that was a nice piece of flying, MJ," Mike repeated.

MJ looked back at him and took another sip of her coffee. "Thanks."

Captain Stewart and Colonel Ferguson took leave of the conference room, followed by another pilot dressed in a flight suit. MJ assumed it was the other F-16 pilot involved in the intercept. The only people left in the room were Gregg Hanscom, Peter Hazleton of the CIA, and MJ.

"More coffee, MJ?" Gregg offered.

"No, thanks. This has to be the first time that I've drunk coffee and it has *stopped* me from shaking, not caused it. However, I've had enough. So tell me again how they knew about us," she said.

"It was sheer luck, mostly," Gregg answered. "A Mexican border patrol unit was checking out possible holding sites for illegal aliens. You know, places where they gather while they wait to cross the border with their coyote. The Mexican unit was patrolling further south than usual, fortunately for us. They came across an old abandoned ranch and noticed there were a lot of fresh tire tracks in the area, so they decided to check it out. It wasn't too difficult to see that something wasn't right. There were car parts dumped behind the house, probably taken from the truck that was supposed to be bringing them to you in Phoenix. Further investigation turned up a car in the barn with a trunk full of bloodstains. There was a gun and some clothing nearby, hidden beneath some old hay. The agents called for backup, and the whole area turned into a treasure hunt. They found a shallow grave just off a secondary road with the bodies of the drivers from the auto plant; a foreman came up and identified them. This led them to the nearest border crossings and conversations with the guards. It was one of the American guards who told us he was suspicious of the two men in the truck headed for Phoenix. He said his supervisor hurried them through, but he didn't like it. That supervisor, by the way, is facing further questioning.

We couldn't believe our luck when the truck showed up at the same border crossing on its way back into Mexico. Maybe they thought it would take a lot longer to discover the switch. They probably thought they would be safe until the truck and drivers were due back at the plant. It took some persuasion for them to give us the information we needed, but we got the one named Rafael to cooperate. He told us about the planned kidnapping in Kansas City; what he did not tell us were the plans for the attack on Chicago. He may not have known about them, though. He gave us the impression they were just moving drugs, nothing more.

It took our agents in Kansas City a while to track down your partner. Someone at the FBO saw two men in company uniforms leave a fuel truck at the wrong end of the airport and get into a car; one man was shoving the other. The witness called the police and gave them a description of the vehicle. Although an immediate APB was issued, it took quite a while to catch up to them. They were heading south on a major highway when a state trooper saw

313

them and called it in. The troopers were able to cut them off and get them stopped; however, the driver held the troopers off by threatening to kill your partner. It took a sharpshooter to end it."

"Is Otto OK?" MJ asked.

"Yes, he's fine. He told us what happened, but he didn't know what was in the containers, either. He thought they were just using you to haul their drugs. We didn't know anything about a gas attack until you told us."

"I wonder why they didn't tell their own people what they were up to?" MJ said, to no one in particular.

"Maybe they needed to keep the lid on it," Gregg offered. "The stakes were pretty high. If the word got back to Chicago as to what the Colombians were trying to do, there would have been a major blood bath on both sides."

"And what about Ned?" she asked.

"Ned has been taken to the psychiatric unit of a local hospital," Peter Hazleton said. "He will remain there until it can be determined if he is competent to stand trial. He was very distraught and incoherent when we pulled him from the plane. Did you know he has cancer?"

"Cancer?" she asked. "He never said anything about being sick, let alone having cancer."

"Our agents have been checking his background around the clock and talking to everyone who has been in contact with him recently. He told his doctor in Mexico that it's a result of his three tours in Vietnam, too much contact with Agent Orange. He's only known about it for the last few months. The doctor told him that it already had a good grip on him, and although the doctor was willing to try and treat it, the prognosis was not good."

"Why would he go through all this trouble and risk if he knew he was probably going to die soon?" she asked.

"Does the name Mariana mean anything to you?" Peter asked.

"Mariana? Yes, sure. I met her in Mexico City, at a restaurant in the hotel where I was staying. He also mentioned her while we were flying to Chicago. He told me that he brought her from this village in Oaxaca to Mexico City a long time ago because an American missionary woman could no longer take care of her. She was an orphan; her parents were dead."

"Well, at least one of them was," Peter said.

"What do you mean, 'one of them'?"

"That's his daughter, MJ. He was probably trying to set something up for her, because he knew he wasn't going to be around much longer to help."

"You've *got* to be kidding! I never knew!" MJ said. "He never gave me a clue the entire year I spent flying with him. I guess there was more to Ned than I thought."

"Apparently. We are still digging into his past. It is quite interesting, to say the least," Gregg said. "What we have found concerning Mariana is that Ned married a local girl from that village near Oaxaca, but she died shortly after Mariana was born. He thought he could use his medical skills to take care of the complications that developed after the birth. She was a very young girl, but infection set in, and they couldn't get medical help fast enough to save her. Ned was devastated. He blamed himself for her death. Mariana still doesn't know that Ned's her father. He doesn't want her to ever know that he is the one responsible for her mother's death. He lost all confidence in his ability to care for anyone, including her. He couldn't deal with the responsibility of raising her, so he made arrangements for others to take care of her. She was raised as an orphan, although she had very loving caretakers along the way. He did a lot for her as she was growing up, but she thinks he's just a friend of the family."

"That's an incredible story. I can't believe he kept that whole thing a secret from me during the time we spent together. In spite of his apparent motivation, I'm sorry to see that he chose to go down this road; I thought he was a great guy. He's helped so many people," she said.

"That will be taken into consideration, MJ," Gregg said. "I don't think you should give up on him entirely. Everyone makes mistakes; I'm just glad this one didn't come to fruition."

"Miss Carlson . . . MJ?" a man said, entering the room abruptly.

"Yes?"

"Telephone," he said.

"Hello?" she said, putting the cell phone to her ear.

"Well, Cap, this is a fine mess you've gotten us into!"

"Otto? Where the hell are you?" she asked. "Are you OK?"

"Yeah, I'm fine, thanks. How about you?" he asked.

"I'm OK. The bird is a bit of a mess, though. How are you at fixing 20mm cannon holes?"

"Key-riced, MJ. You really know how to hurt a guy."

"You'll have to remove approach lights and fixtures from the flight surfaces and fuselage, too. It looks like you've got your work cut out for you, Ottoman."

"You've got to learn to take better care of your equipment, MJ, especially if you plan to make any money at this flying business thing. Tell you what: I will fix your plane if you pay for my dinner."

"Excuse me?" Where the hell are you, Otto?"

"Juanito's Corral in Phoenix. They just served me a nice plateful of carnitas."

"You went there without me, you Hog? That's the last time I tell *you*

319

about any of my secret eating
places!"

"Well, you *did* forget to tell me
about their margaritas, MJ. They are
absolutely the bomb. I'm on my third
one!"

"Poor choice of adjectives, Otto."

"Meaning?"

"Forget it! I'll fill you in
later. Why don't you have a couple
more, then you won't need a plane to
get up here; you can levitate."

"I plan on it, Boss. I've booked a
flight to Chicago that leaves in two
hours; you *know* I can't fly with
those guys sober."

"Once a freight dog, always a
freight dog, eh Archie?"

"Archibald to you, Captain Mary
Jane Carlson. And, yes, as always,
you are right. ARRRROOOOOOOOOOO!" he
howled.

MJ held the telephone away from
her ear and laughed, as the
bewildered faces around her focused

on the haunting sound that poured
from the receiver.

"*Too* much!"

Printed in the United States
1092200001B/106-216